LUSCIOUS

Stories of Anal Eroticism

Also edited by Alison Tyler

Best Bondage Erotica
Best Bondage Erotica 2
Heat Wave: Sizzling Sex Stories
The Merry XXXmas Book of Erotica
Three-Way: Erotic Stories

LUSCIOUS

Stories of Anal Eroticism

EDITED BY ALISON TYLER
FOREWORD BY TRISTAN TAORMINO

CLEIS
PRESS

Published in the United States by Cleis Press Inc.,
P.O. Box 14697, San Francisco, California 94114.

Printed in the United States.
Cover design: Scott Idleman
Cover photograph: Lucien Clergue/Getty Images
Book design: Karen Quigg
Cleis Press logo art: Juana Alicia
First Edition.
10 9 8 7 6 5 4 3 2 1

To SAM. Always.

Forbidden fruit a flavor has
That lawful orchards mocks;
How luscious lies the pea within
The pod that Duty locks!

—EMILY DICKINSON (1830-86)

Acknowledgments

Many thanks to Violet Blue for promoting the concept of rimming (as well as all other things deliciously oral) on her exquisite website www.tinynibbles.com. Miss Blue has a knack for making sexual pleasure seem like a God-given right. She rocks my world, and she knows it. (Plus she's a kick-ass webmistress and she's gorgeous to boot!)

Applause to the breathtaking Tristan Taormino for being an anal sex pioneer. Her book *The Ultimate Guide to Anal Sex for Women* is stellar (as is Bill Brent's *The Ultimate Guide to Anal Sex for Men*) and her video versions of the book contain some of the hottest anal sex around!

Two thumbs up to Carol Queen for *Bend Over Boyfriend,* a video classic delightfully featured in one of the stories in this book.

A nod to the writers of *Sex and the City* for the episodes exploring anal sex and rimming. Many of my more vanilla friends (along with my cousin's wife!) have confessed to me that they were finally able to broach the subject of anal sex with their partners after viewing these episodes.

Thanks to *Bridget Jones's Diary* for the hinting at a bout of anal sex between the characters played by Hugh Grant and Renée Zellweger. Thanks also to the Marquis de Sade (I first read about anal sex in *The 120 Days of Sodom*), and to Scott Turow (or maybe I first read about it in *Presumed Innocent*), and Anne Rice (for making anal sex, enemas, and butt plugs seem so undeniably pretty in her Sleeping Beauty trilogy).

Thanks to The Doors for singing "Back Door Man" and to No Doubt for "Hey Baby" (I know I'm purposely misunderstanding the lyrics, but I don't care).

Thank you to the ever-remarkable Felice Newman and Frédérique Delacoste for letting me take on this project and run with it.

And thank you to SAM for not saying no.

Contents

FOREWORD: ASS FANTASY

Tristan Taormino

From *Ass Worship* to *Anal Expedition*, one look at the best-selling porn titles in any given month, and the trend is clear: when folks have a choice of big-budget features, threesomes, interracial sex, amateurs, eighteen year olds, MILFs, and nearly every other sexual niche imaginable, they choose anal movies. And it's not just pornophiles either. From magazines to self-help books, anal sex is always high on the list of people's fantasies. It's one of the most frequently searched-for terms on the Web. So what is it about behinds and banging them that gets us so hot and bothered? I've got a few theories.

The ass has been eroticized for centuries. We can all agree that a butt's something to check out as it walks by in tight jeans, pat gently in admiration, squeeze on the sly, cup firmly when you've got a mouthful of pussy or cock, or dig your heels into while you're getting fucked. What lies between the cheeks can be a source of incredible pleasure and while the notion of the ass as an erogenous zone in its own right is not new, the public discussion of it is.

For such a tight-lipped little area, the butthole says a whole lot about American culture. With nicknames ranging from flowery (rosebud) to filthy (poop chute), the brown eye is full of complexity and contradiction. It represents strength and control to some and ultimate vulnerability to others. It's delicate yet resilient and embodies some of our deepest needs—things like privacy, trust, and power. Some fear it, others fetishize it, and everyone has to think about it on a regular basis. Talk of it can elicit feelings from stress to silliness. What other hole do you know that is associated with Freudian pathology, puritanical repression, and homophobia? That's one busy orifice.

While it symbolizes some of our fundamental fixations, it transcends another of our collective obsessions: gender. In this age of gender fluidity and transgendered bodies, the ass emerges as a kind of neutral territory of the flesh, the ultimate genderless (or multigendered) erogenous zone. While genderqueers attempt to reimagine, reclaim, even rename sites of pleasure like breasts, cunts, and cocks that are heavily identified as male or female, the ass is everyman's hole—a source of pleasure unencumbered by society's gender roles and expectations.

Why we fantasize about anal sex reveals just how powerful and varied its meanings are. To lots of people, anal sex is unattainable in a no-means-you-are-never-ever-going-there-honey kind of way. We want it because it's out of our reach. It turns us on like banging the boss's hot wife, doing Angelina Jolie, or having a threesome with them both—precisely because it ain't gonna happen.

In addition to wanting what we can't have, we're aroused by what we're not supposed to do—the thing that would shock our friends and neighbors at church if they found out we did it. We like to misbehave, especially when it comes to sex. Anal sex fulfills our desire to be the sexual rebel, to stray from convention, to be, quite simply, naughty.

Ass-fucking does not just challenge societal norms, it can also be a way to test the limits of the body. You can ask an awful lot of a very small opening (think anal fisting up to the elbow). For the segment of the population who like to see how far they can push their bodies, anal sex can be an extreme sport for the bedroom. One of the most popular subjects of letters I receive is about those limits, with questions like: How wide is too wide? How long can a toy be? How much can I fit in my ass? Some people don't necessarily want to actually do it, but they want to fantasize about doing it or watch someone else do it. The rising popularity of anal sex videos that feature gaping (where, after lots of penetration, the anus is wide open), shows the appeal of imagery that depicts how far our bodies can go.

When all you hear is dick-pussy this and dick-pussy that, the ass remains neglected and overlooked, but this contributes to it having a mysterious quality. For that *Star Trek* fan in us all, there's excitement in the element of darkness, the unknown, the mystique of a place where no one has gone before. It's our frontier-exploring, cowboy spirit that yearns to make the tough journey, then stick our flagpole in it to mark our territory.

It's no secret I love anal sex, in real life and as fantasy material (yes, I admit I fast-forward straight to the buttfucking). For me, it's all about power and consciousness. I think that every sexual exchange is a power exchange and playing with that dynamic is what can make sex extraordinary. Anal sex is the perfect vehicle for dominance and submission play since so much of it can be about control and surrender. Because of the way it has been represented (often as violent) and the fact that you could actually hurt someone if you don't do it right, there is a sense of danger swirling around ass-play. On top of that, it's not exactly something most people can just *do*. Very few performers can phone in an anal scene in a video and nonprofessionals need time, preparation, and a whole lot more for it to work. That's why anal sex can generate a greater sense of self-awareness and give people the opportunity to really engage with their own bodies and with one another.

The growing popularity of that puckered hole and where it leads is undeniable. The fact that it means so many different things to different people reveals just how multifaceted one sex act can be. Anal sex represents the ultimate collision between public and private, where a person gets to go inside another's deepest, darkest place to feel it and to know it through an erotic act laced with cultural taboos (more so than other acts). It's rich territory for writers.

This is the first collection of multisexual anal-themed erotica that I know of, which raises the question: What took us so long? With plenty of books of BDSM erotica, vampire erotica, and even lesbian cowboy erotica to fill our shelves, it's amazing that an all-anal-all-the-time anthology is just now making its debut. It's a debut not just long overdue, but important. In most Hollywood movies and mainstream media, buttfucking is still shown as violent and degrading—or it's the punch line of a quick joke and nothing more.

In print, this subset of fantasies has been mostly relegated to porno mags. Sure, stories featuring backdoor romps have appeared in other erotica anthologies, but to organize a book around the theme of ass love drives home the point that this is not just the fly-by-night fantasy of a few, nor is it one specifically concocted by and for men. A book like this one expands the erotic representations of a still-mythologized and misunderstood sexual experience. It gives context and color to a sex menu item that is too frequently painted as one dimensional. It gives voice to women's butt fantasies, of which we have not heard enough. It illustrates the depth, variety, and intensity of anal pleasure—not to mention its unquestionable jerk-off potential.

Tristan Taormino
New York City
October 2005

INTRODUCTION

I am one of those individuals who believes that between two (or three, four, or five) consenting adults, anything goes. But that doesn't mean I think all sex acts are created equal. Recently, I annoyed a sex-positive editor friend of mine by casually referring to the act of anal sex as "dirty" in one of my stories.

"It's not dirty!" she insisted, outraged, as she cut the line from the piece. "It's a beautiful, loving act between two special people."

Sure it is.

But to me, it's also dirty. And I don't mean that in a bad way. Because *dirty* can be exquisite. Dirty can be luscious. Dirty can make what you do between the rumpled white sheets, or under the sun-washed bleachers, or in the darkened parking lot that much more arousing.

In my first novel, written way back when I was twenty-two, I provided a description of two people engaged in foreplay that included some casual line about rimming. My male roommate shared this passage with one of his buddies, who decided to quote the sentence back to me at a bar. "I nibbled slowly around her asshole," this handsome dark-haired man whispered under his breath to me in the gold-speckled, late afternoon light at El Coyote.

"Excuse me?" My cheeks were as hot as the homemade salsa on the table.

"You wrote that," he said, his voice dangerously husky. "Didn't you?"

Yeah, I did. So why was I blushing? Because hearing the words echoed back to me—in the middle of a Hollywood Happy Hour, no less—made them seem indescribably dirty. Heart pounding, panties wet, I nodded.

"So *did* he?"

"Did he *what*?"

"Nibble around your—" the man whispered.

I was saved from answering by another round of tequila shots. But thinking back on that night, I know that if he'd recited a line of mine about two people simply fucking, I wouldn't have been nearly as scarlet-cheeked. Fact is, there are just some ways people play that hit the dirty note in my mind. And those are my favorite acts.

When I pick up a book of erotica, I don't want to read about "beautiful" and "loving." I want to read about sweaty and heart-stopping. About gently parting a lover's dimpled rear cheeks and peeking between them. About bringing your tongue ever so slowly to that valley and licking up and around, sweetly, seductively. About giving yourself over to that sensuous act and knowing that you're as hot or hard or wet as you are, precisely *because* it is so fucking dirty.

Just like the stories in this collection.

My goal when putting together this anthology was to include a tantalizing array of tales that dealt with the many erotic aspects of anal play across gender lines. Variety is definitely the spice of anal sex, and I wanted to feature stories that used fingers and tongues, real cocks and silicone phalluses, beads and vibrators. I also wanted to explore the different rhythms of anal sex, from the delicious foreplay of light teasing to the ferociousness of slamming all the way in. From short (although not necessarily sweet), as in "Off the Rim" by Ayre Riley to long and dreamily detailed, as in one of my all-time favorite anal sex stories, "Selling Point" by Carl Kennedy.

I hoped to hear about novices (like the lover in Dante Davidson's confessional "Antonia's Beast") and longtime players (like the narrator in Kate Dominic's "Trophy Wife"). And I wanted to read stories from writers who feel like anal sex is just another sexy way to play, as well as from those who like to think the act is as erotically naughty as I do (check out Erica Dumas's "Something Dirty"). But though the stories in this book are wildly different, they do have one important thing in common. From Shanna Germain's oh-so-arousing "Cherry Bottom" to Lavie Tidhar's inspired poem "Anal Sex in Montmartre" the pieces in this book meet the title's demands. They are, simply put: luscious.

Alison Tyler
September 2005

CHERRY BOTTOM

Shanna Germain

"You okay, babe?" Andrew's voice above me was half sexual rasp, half concern. His warm, oiled hands had moved from the outside curves of my ass to the inside of my thighs, and they were resting there, not pulling or teasing, just resting against my skin. I kept my eyes and mouth closed and tried not to think about my naked ass in the air. I nodded against the pillow.

"She'll tell you if she's not," Miss Suzanne's voice came from the other side of me. "Won't you, Cate?" I nodded again, the rustle of the pillow filling my ear. Miss Suzanne pressed her cool, slim fingers next to Andrew's, higher up on the inside of my thigh. The hot and cold of their hands made my ass break out in goose bumps. "See, Andrew? She'll tell you. So stop stalling."

Miss Suzanne's fingers left my skin. Her heels *click-clicked* away, presumably to another one of the six couples where the husband was also stalling.

Andrew's hands didn't move. I waited, head on my hands, belly and thighs resting on the prop-up pillow, ass in the air. My bare body still had goose bumps, although the room was warm enough. Some of it was anticipation. But most of it was fear— Miss Suzanne's anal sex class was our last resort. If we couldn't get Andrew over his fear of anal sex here, I was afraid it was never going to happen.

It had been difficult enough to ask for it—the way I was brought up, girls aren't supposed to like any sex. And they definitely aren't supposed to like it the way I liked it. And poor Andrew—he wanted so badly to please me, but he couldn't get over his fear of hurting me. No matter how many times I told him, no matter how much I begged for it. We'd tried videos and books. I'd even bought the smallest butt plug at the store. It was straw-sized, really, but still, he couldn't bring himself to put it inside me. Not even just a little bit. *Bad experience,* was all he'd say. But this class had been his gift to me, and I knew he wanted to please me, even if he was afraid. So now here we were, being taught anal sex by Miss Suzanne Saunders, southern belle turned sex therapist. Our first two classes had been lectures and book learning. Today was hands-on. Today was our last chance.

I concentrated on letting my muscles go loose, on breathing in through my nose. We'd just spent ten minutes playing, getting warmed up. A little strange, to share foreplay in front of the dozen other people in the room, but every time I looked up, they were all concentrating on their own space, their own bodies. It was like a yoga class in the nude. And despite his fears about anal, Andrew didn't seem to have any fears about public sex. He just ran his tongue up and down between my thighs, reached up and ran his wet thumb over and over my nipple until I could only lean back and try to keep my moans quiet.

I wanted this so badly, I could almost feel him inside me, the fullness of him, the weight. The way his balls would slap against me. Jesus, it had been so long, I could barely remember how it felt. I took a deep breath and tried to think of something else for a minute, tried to be calm so that Andrew would be calm.

Andrew's fingers held steady at the inside of my thigh, one second, two. Then he ran them up through the crack between my cheeks. With one hand, he spread my asscheeks open. With the other, he circled the skin around my asshole. Part of our class had been learning the anatomy of the asshole, getting used to its pink pucker, its hairless expanse of membrane. Knowing that Andrew was looking at me like that, that he was studying me, made my pussy ache for his fingers. My asshole too. I wanted to reach my fingers underneath me, to ease the ache in my clit, but we weren't supposed to move, so I squeezed my eyes more tightly shut and tried to enjoy the ache. Maybe I could learn something too.

Andrew's finger went around and around, in tighter and tighter circles toward my asshole. The tip of his finger ran against it and I could barely breathe. I wanted him, any part of him inside me so bad. He held his finger there, not moving it in or out...just resting his finger against it like it was a button he was deciding whether or not to press.

Miss Suzanne's heels *click-clicked* toward the front of the room. "Okay, ladies and gentlemen, I want you to get your fingers really well lubed, the way we talked about earlier. We're going in."

The class broke into nervous giggles. I was glad to hear Andrew's snort, the same one he gave at the comic strips at home. But his finger at my ass didn't move. Against my legs, his thigh muscles tightened.

*C'mon, baby. C'mon...*mental telepathy, the only encouragement I could offer him. I hoped he could hear. That he could hear me begging, could hear how much I wanted him like this.

Click-click: Miss Suzanne and her heels again, right at our table. "Can I help, Andrew?" she asked. He must have said yes, because then her cool fingers were at my asscheeks again, spreading them for him. My asshole puckered up against the cold. My tightening nipples crinkled the paper sheet beneath me.

Andrew's fingers left my body, came back oiled and warm.

"It's like playing pool," Miss Suzanne said, her thin fingers still in place. "It's all about speed and angles." Andrew's finger was back against me, pressing, pressing. I fought the desire to lean back onto the tip of his finger, to force him inside me once and for all. But part of our class promise had been to let our partner do all the work, at his own pace; let him do only what he was ready for.

He increased the pressure, opening my asshole, careful to use the flat of his fingertip. "Go," Miss Suzanne whispered, and then Andrew pushed his way inside me. Just a little, just the tip so I could barely feel it, but oh Jesus, there he was.

"More," Miss Suzanne said. Andrew pushed his finger farther into my asshole. Farther, until I was sure he had to be at the first joint. Having him in there like that made my pussy ache with that special emptiness that I loved. Andrew entered me to the knuckle. I imagined what he looked like behind me—starting to sweat beneath his glasses out of fear and excitement, his finger disappearing into my asshole.

"All the way in," Miss Suzanne said. And then he pushed and his finger was inside me, tearing through me with that certain pain that is mostly pleasure. I bit down on the pillow, but most of the moan came out anyway.

"See?" Miss Suzanne said. "She likes it. You're doing a great job."

"Jesus," Andrew whispered. "Oh fuck." Awe and arousal deepened his voice to a husky whisper. Hearing that voice—with no fear in it—almost made me come.

Miss Suzanne raised her voice. "Okay, class, is everyone in? Foxes all in the holes?" I'm sure the class laughed, but I couldn't even concentrate to hear all the answers. All I could feel was Andrew's finger in my ass, the way he held it there, so still, the way it filled me and at the same time made me ache for something more, something bigger.

"Great," she said. "Now I just want you to wiggle your fingers in there a little bit. Not a lot, just enough to feel the room, to see what kind of reaction you get."

This time, Andrew didn't hesitate. As soon as she said wiggle, his finger started moving, up and down, up and down, inside me.

"Okay?" Andrew asked. But this time he wasn't asking if I was okay. He was asking if it felt good, if he was doing the right thing in there.

My voice was all whisper from the effort of not fucking his finger. "Yes," I said. "Yes, please don't stop."

Miss Suzanne *click-clicked* back to the front of the room, apparently trusting that Andrew had gotten the hang of things.

After a few minutes she said, "Ladies, now it's your turn to help out. Gentlemen, your job is just to hold yourself still. Maybe for the first time ever, your ladies are going to fuck you."

Andrew's finger stopped moving in my ass. Light-headed, I pushed myself backward onto Andrew's finger, so far back his other curled knuckles rubbed against my skin. I let myself fuck him, showing him how much I wanted him like this, how much I wanted him inside me.

With each thrust, Andrew's breathing quickened. His finger burned and rubbed the inside of me in pain and pleasure. I was so full back there that the rest of me ached, empty and untouched. With one hand, I reached beneath me and fingered my slippery clit, letting everything build inside me. The fullness and the emptiness. The sweet burn of Andrew's finger in my ass, the soft roll of pleasure through my clit. And the best part was Andrew behind me, bracing himself against the table, letting me fuck him, I hoped, without fear for the first time. Seeing there was no pain, that there was only pleasure.

I was close to coming, but I wasn't sure if we were supposed to, if we'd been given the go-ahead, or if there was more I was supposed to do. And then Andrew moved his finger inside me, up and down, just enough to hit that spot and it didn't matter if I was supposed to or not, it was happening. Everything sliding through me from Andrew's finger out to my toes, up into my head. I cried out, and heard Andrew do the same.

I pulled forward off of Andrew's finger, and let my head hang on the pillow. "Holy shit," I said. I had no idea where anyone else was at in the room, or if there even was anyone else in the room anymore. And then I heard Miss Suzanne's heels *click-click* up. "Once you two have washed up, meet me in the front room to debrief and get your assignments for next week." She put her hand, still cool as ever, against my shoulder. "Nice job, you two."

When I sat up, Andrew's face was pink and flushed. But he had the biggest grin on his face. Just seeing him like that, aroused and confident, made me wet all over again. He leaned down and kissed my earlobe. "That," he whispered, "was awesome. I can't wait to see what our next assignment is."

I thought of his cock, the tip of it entering me, the way it would feel when he finally pushed inside of me. "I can't either."

THE HOLE
THAT I HAVE

Joy St. James

*You go to war with the Army you have, not the Army
you may wish you have.*
— SECRETARY OF DEFENSE DONALD RUMSFELD,
SPEAKING TO THE TROOPS IN IRAQ, 2005

Men are clueless. Most men, anyway; there are always excep-
tions. Take my old best boyfriend, for example. He's an
exception. He knows me so well. He prefers ass-fucking. That's
why he likes special girls like me. But this isn't about him.

This is about most men, who, as I say, are totally clueless.
Most of them would "fuck a venetian blind," as Nora Ephron
so eloquently put it. Perversely perhaps, these are the very men
I crave: horny straight guys. Their pussy-poking penises, though
indiscriminate, validate me as a woman.

Last night is a perfect example: I'm with this guy I just met.
We're going at it hot and heavy, kissing like mad. Though we've

still got our clothes on, he's somehow managed to unhook my bra so that his hands can play with my well-developed titties. Then he's on top of me and spreads my legs apart. While he humps away, I retrieve a lubricated condom, the kind I always keep tucked in my panty hose under the elastic waistband. I can feel his hard cock rubbing up against his zipper just dying to get out, free at last, and into my hole.

"Oh, baby," he moans. "I want you."

Excitedly, he fumbles with his zipper. Just as excitedly—indeed, enthusiastically and eagerly—I rip off the condom wrapper. His cock pops out. I can feel the clear but gooey precum as I deftly slide the rubber on. He doesn't object. In fact, he's hardly conscious of what's happening, as his brain is now firmly in his penis. All he can do is grind and pump with his cock just looking for a home. A home, and just about any old hole will do.

As he unzips my skirt and starts tugging at my panty hose to get at my cunt, I whisper in his ear: "Oh, sweetie, I want you to ravish me with my clothes on. It's so sexy that way."

"Whatever you say, baby. I just want to fuck you. I need to slide my cock into your cunt."

"Me, too." I giggle. "My hungry cunt so needs your throbbing cock deep, deep inside me." Again I giggle, now at my own purple prose.

I reach my hands under my butt, and with one of my sculpted nails, make an incision in my panty hose right where my asshole is. (Don't worry: it's not like they're Wolford's hosiery or anything pricey like that!) Then my hands tug at the rip to make sure it's big enough while at the same time sliding my panties to expose my asshole.

Now comes the tricky part: my fingers find the rim of the Vaseline-coated butt plug I always insert into my asshole before each maybe-I'll-get-lucky date. It sounds so premeditated and clinical, doesn't it? But every girl knows that carefully making oneself alluringly ready for sex—the anticipation—can be as fun as the actual sex itself, right? So it is that my little girlie thingie makes me feel so full and fuckable.

Girlie thingie sounds better than butt plug, doesn't it? It's my version of a tampon. A kind of secret code that only real females can understand. And it'll remain our little secret, okay? Just between us girls. It's always better for the guys to remain clueless. They're embarrassed even to buy tampons when a girlfriend asks it as a favor when they go the store. I remember I was embarrassed, too, the very first time. It was a rite of passage, making me a woman (makeup and a dress weren't enough). I even remember I bought a bunch of other girlie things—Yoplait yogurt, *Self* magazine, L'eggs panty hose—so the big box of Easy Glide would be kind of camouflaged, perfectly natural. Still, I couldn't help but be nervous and self-conscious as the checkout clerk seemed to stare at me. Naturally, the clerk was a woman; a guy would never have read me.

When I got home, I immediately started experimenting: What would it feel like, I wondered, to have a foreign presence inside me, up my ass? Would it hurt or feel good—or hurt so good? The plastic applicator, too hard, and my will for self-inflicted pain, too weak? I tried and tried, but it only brought frustration—and tears to my eyes. Maybe I wasn't really meant to be a girl after all? Finally, after I'd dipped the applicator in gobs and gobs of Vaseline, it worked its way in. And when my thumb pushed the end of the applicator to inject the exploding cotton tampon with its spermlike tail, I discovered what happiness could be, what it meant to be filled. My true destiny was confirmed: to make myself as femininely sexy as possible so as to make cocks turn hard, all the better to service me, to plug my one hole, always inviting, ever receptive to moments like this.

With a gentle tug, the butt plug's out, and my hole is primed for his nice hard cock. The guy, of course, never notices. I discreetly drop the butt plug on the floor, to be gathered up afterward, along with my bra. When he's rolled off me, limp and spent and about to lapse into a satisfied snooze, only then will I scamper to the bathroom to take care of my girlie thingie, hidden from his view, cupped in my hand.

Finally ready, I throw my legs over his shoulders and take his cock in my hand, showing it the way home through my torn panty hose and into my hole. I rock my hips just so, to help the head of his penis punch through. That always hurts a bit, I must confess, even for a well-practiced anal slut like me. But once that barrier is breached, everything else feels easy; so wonderfully, pleasurably easy it's not at all unnatural or weird or sinful or anything bad like that. Rather, it was meant to be. There's happiness in that, fulfilling my destiny. And fulfillment in the extraordinary fullness of being I now feel: the hard cock so deep inside me, I feel as though I can taste it—a kind of reverse deep throat, my other favorite way of taking cock.

He thrusts and pounds away. His words sound guttural: "Oh, baby, you're so tight. I love your cunt."

Each powerful thrust takes my breath away, so my words come out in gasps: "And my cunt adores your cock, my sexy sweetie."

He pumps harder, faster, more furiously now. Except for involuntary groans and grunts of pleasure, he's silent. About to come, I think. But typically, hopefully, he doesn't come, not right then anyway, so quickly, so unsatisfactorily. Instead, he lasts and lasts, which is just what I want, hard and deep inside filling me up forever. It always helps that he has had a few drinks, not so many as to interfere with his cock's performance, of course, but just enough to make him last and last. And just enough, of course, so that he never notices a girl's flaws!

"Harder, harder," I plead. "Fuck me harder!"

And he does. He gives me just what I want: a hard cock inside me that makes me complete, a woman in full. When he finally does come, it's like my whole alimentary canal goes into spasm. And what a deliriously delightful and delicious trembling it is. I moan and shriek. He thinks I'm coming, too. Which is a good thing, right?

Afterward, he invariably says something like: "Wow! That's one of the best fucks I've ever had. Your cunt is so tight." Then the inevitable question: "Was it good for you, too?"

"You don't know how good." I giggle. Men are so insecure, I feel compelled to keep babbling on: "You're such a stud! That cock of yours is just so incredible, so big, I can't describe how wonderful it made my cunt feel. We're a perfect fit, don't you think, your huge cock and my tight cunt."

He nods and grins ear to ear. But if he knew the truth? Knew that I had really not had an orgasm? Knew that what he assumed was vaginal sex was really anal sex? He would probably strangle me. It's not unheard of, you know, for a straight guy to physically abuse or even kill a transsexual woman who has fooled him. But I never dare let my pretty little head get filled with evil thoughts like that. Getting filled with a nice hard cock is all I let myself think about.

And even when he finally leaves, I'm still thinking about it. In fact, now I'm nice and primed and ready to come myself. That's when, now all alone, I take out my special sex toy, the scorpion. Its flexible plastic tail sticks into my ass, and its pincers clasp around my big clit. Attached is a long cord to a handheld control that makes the scorpion vibrate at my whim. I gradually turn it up to top speed. Its tail squirming in my now sensitized ass brings new and different pleasures from the cock just recently inside me. And the scorpion's pincers around my own cocklike clit vibrate too, making me hard. Not really hard like when I was a guy, but only slightly firm because of all the girlie hormones I've dosed on over the years, now coursing through my body. Likewise, when I orgasm, a big wad of come no longer shoots out; rather, it's just a little squirt, an estrogen-diluted dribble.

But, wow! What an orgasm it is, this fantasy fuck. As I linger and luxuriate in the remembered feeling of his, the latest and oh-so-real cock deep inside me, I feel as though I'm having multiple orgasms, and each one, I promise, is better, so much better, than when I was "fully functional." Even a genetic girl, a true cunt, couldn't ask for anything more.

Ravished and spent, I look in the mirror next to the bed. I can see myself through the eyes of an equally spent guy, my imaginary lover: I see a hungry cunt who's finally been satisfied. I draw my hands up to my breasts and feel my still-hard nipples, then pucker my lips to throw a kiss toward the mirror. Yes, I'm a girl, a happy girl who's just been fucked.

I used to assume, just assume, that I'd get genital surgery one day. But now I wonder. Who needs it? Who needs a real cunt when I've got a perfectly good, wonderfully serviceable, cumhole already? As long as I'm getting fucked, who cares? The guys certainly don't. And so they become my dream merchants: their cocks inside me make me a girl.

For girls who were born girls, who take their cunts for granted, anal sex is simply a choice. For me, it's a necessity, and therefore it seems so much sexier, the only way to get fucked and filled with what I need. What's a girl to do when she doesn't have a cunt? You must fuck with the hole that you have.

But my girlfriends think I'm deceitful, that I should tell a guy up front that I'm not a GG (genetic girl), like lucky them, but a shemale bottom.

"That's no fun," I say. "I would never get as much straight cock."

Then they always want to know details, lots and lots of juicy details, about my latest adventures in anal sex. Of course, I tell them. We're intimate, we share secrets. Girl talk. I'm accepted, part of the group, one of the girls. Just another cunt, as a guy would say.

EDWARD'S EXPERIMENTS

Saskia Walker

Life with Edward is never dull. He isn't the sort of man you'd immediately assume is a sex stud, but he is, in his own unique way. He's quietly attractive in a lean, studious manner. He comes from a long line of scientists and he's a scientist through and through. His field of expertise is researching insect behavior and translating the data to inform large-scale robotics design. Geeky? Maybe. But hear me out.

Edward has an insatiable curiosity about how things work. That makes every day with him a vivid exploration of life's possibilities. Even a visit to the supermarket has him deeply analyzing packaging mechanisms, products, and ingredients. He picks items out of the basket as I put them in, his eyebrows lifting as he describes the processes used to create his favorite taco sauce. You might think it sounds boring, but no, he's never boring, because he expresses things in such a wacky way, gesticulating to demonstrate, his enthusiasm contagious. Being with Edward is a voyage of discovery. I admit that in the beginning I did think being with such an oddly intense personality might get difficult, or dull. But how wrong could I be?

You see, Edward's curiosity and his yen for experimentation spills over into our sex life. And that more than makes up for his geekiness. To Edward sexual intercourse isn't simply about makin' lurve to his woman, it's an experiment in what's possible and the extent of those possibilities. And I'm on the receiving end. Oh yeah. Now you see where I'm coming from!

Mathematics, chemistry, and physics, they all play their part—sometimes geography too. And human biology comes as a side order with them all.

Mathematics most recently came into play when his challenge was to "empty the box." He wanted to find out if he could work his way through a packet of condoms in one session, thereby testing his own limits as well as my capacity for pleasure. He told me of this intention over dinner, quite seriously, pulling out a three-pack, a six-pack, and a twelve-pack. He set them down on the table between us.

I smiled and tried not to look too eager. "Go for it."

He did.

Edward's wiry and fit—he plays squash and cycles daily—so stamina has never been an issue. The first night of the experiment he got through the three-pack. He paced himself throughout the whole procedure, ripping off the used rubber after ejaculating and rolling another straight on as he plowed back into me, hardly missing a beat. Multiple orgasm hit me at the start of the third go-round. I was a puddle of bliss on the bed.

The next week he insisted on trying for the six-pack. He emptied the box that time too, filling the last one a supreme effort in willpower that left me whimpering for mercy. Afterward, when he was deep in slumber, his limbs were still twitching from the extreme effort he'd sustained for so long.

I refused to let him go for the twelve-pack. I thought he was too young to die.

Chemistry? That one was interesting.

"I'm taking you for a special dinner at The Olive Tree tonight." The glint in his eyes told me he had something planned. When didn't he?

"You are?"

"Yes, and I'd like you to wear your short velvet dress and...stockings."

The Olive Tree is an expensive place with plush booths and a menu to die for. I dressed while he lay on the bed watching, my anticipation for whatever it was he had in mind building by the moment. I love surprises. Which was just as well. Before I'd even finished dressing he got up and stalked over to me, hitched my dress up around my hips, put his hand inside my G-string and massaged my clit until I was shuddering with pleasure.

"What are you doing?" I moaned while I clutched him with one stacked heel lifted from the floor to give his hand better access.

"Wait and see," he said, his flashing eyes sending a tremor right through me. After I'd peaked and begun to calm he pulled his wet fingers out of my panties, then drew them along my pulse points: behind my ears, in my cleavage and on my wrists, spreading my juices onto the skin there.

"You've made me wonder what this is about," I said and chuckled, knowing he'd give me an explanation if I actually asked for it.

He moved closer, rubbing up against me, breathing the scent of my spent passion on my warm skin. "The smell of an aroused woman," he whispered, in between planting kisses on my neck. "I want to breathe you in throughout dinner. I want to find out what sort of effect it has on me."

Hell yeah, it had an effect! When we got to the restaurant he kept sliding over to me in the luxurious leather banquette, running his nose up the length of my neck, kissing me in my cleavage—regardless of the surprised stares we received from onlookers—the lust in his expression blatant.

When he finally got me home he threw me on the sofa while the front door was still closing behind us. He pounced on me and went at it like a man possessed. Manhandling my body, changing position constantly, he was on fire.

At one point he was kneeling with my bottom resting in his lap, his cock wedged deep inside me, moving my legs around as if they were antennas and he was trying for better TV reception. It was too good. The extended anticipation he'd endured made him last and last. I came three times before he finally let rip.

Oh, and the physics, yes.

"I want you to masturbate for me. Do it honey, I want to watch...."

Fair enough. That was a common enough request.

"...and then I want to try something else, afterward, to see if there's a difference for you."

"Ah, I see."

Edward's attention is so much fun. I was on my back and performing in a flash. He licked my clit between my fingers while I masturbated, glancing up at my face and watching my expression.

"What now?" I panted, after I'd come.

"I'd like you to do it again, sitting on the washer while it spins." He wanted to know if women really did get a sexual thrill from sitting on a washing machine during the spin cycle. "Have you ever done that before?"

"No, but I'm willing." I laughed at the idea of it. It really wasn't something I'd ever thought about.

We ran downstairs, bubbling with laughter, and he chased me into the kitchen, capturing me in his arms for a sudden sweet kiss.

"You're a very wicked man," I teased.

"No I'm not, I'm just curious." He looked at me meaningfully with his big soulful brown eyes. He really meant it, bless him.

The midafternoon sunlight flooded the kitchen. I was already warm and mellow and I smiled to myself while he programmed the machine. He scooted a basket of linens off the surface and helped me mount the great white beast. It was whirring, readying for the spin cycle. When I got into position the sun hit my back and I purred with pleasure. He moved into the shadow I created, standing between my open legs where they were dangling from the machine, smiling his naughty smile, pushing my hand back in between my thighs.

I began rubbing, quickly keying my senses again after the last time. The machine started to spin. The sensation vibrated right through my pelvis, sending hot waves of pleasure from my clit through my groin to rocket up my spine. The warm spot on my back seemed to mark meltdown point.

I grabbed onto his shoulder with my free hand to steady myself. His gaze went from my face to my jiggling breasts. He held them, molding them in his hands, plucking my nipples. I was gone—my mouth opened, releasing a loud, juddering moan and I came in a series of bone-melting jolts.

As you might imagine, that wasn't the end of that experiment, because Edward had gotten so hot watching he had to do some "debriefing" of his own, right there and then, up against the machine.

Edward does his research about sex and sexuality on his lunch breaks, while eating his high-protein meal and downing an energy drink. When particular things catch his attention he comes home with that lively glint in his eyes. He keeps a logbook of his findings—yes! If he has the energy after an "experiment," he jots notes while I collapse for sleep. He cuddles up to me, promising to turn his notes into a proper report the next day. Satiated and exhausted, I murmur words of love and appropriate encouragement while I pull my delicious scientific stud closer against me.

He says he's going to publish his sex research one day and dedicate it to me. He calls me his muse. Hell, he could call me his lab rat and I wouldn't care! I doubt there's a woman in our town that could claim such attentions as I get from Edward. A beatific smile appears on my face at the very thought of Edward's experiments. The best part of all is that I can't predict them. Although I do grow attentive when he gets that look in his eyes.

"I want to explore the territory of your body."

"Oh, but you do, darling, you do."

"No, I mean I want to know its geography as a whole."

"Go on…"

"Your sensitive, responsive places…your clit, your pussy, your anus… I want to stimulate them all at once, and…I want to watch."

I lifted my eyebrows. "All at once and watch? Is that possible?"

"I think I've worked out a way."

I didn't doubt it for a minute.

But what Edward wasn't expecting was that he'd lose control of this particular experiment. Not only would I turn into a wild animal in heat, he himself would be on the receiving end of so much stimulation he would hardly be capable of analyzing it.

He made me comfy on the bed, propped me up with pillows and put a towel and lots of playthings nearby. He already had an erection but he wouldn't let me toy with it in case it distracted him from the experiment. Hah! Little did he know what was about to occur.

He started me off with some hands-on attention, then employed my favorite vibrator with the diving dolphin clit sleeve. He lubed it up and eased it inside my hungry pussy, murmuring his desire all the while—my researcher was on the case every which way. Making sure it was buried deep, he wedged the dolphin over my clit and then switched that sucker on. Oh boy! He moved it real slow, sliding it in and out—and rocking it barely back and forth—just the way I like it. (NB: result of a previous experiment.)

"That looks so good," he whispered.

His cock was ramrod straight and oozing, he was more than ready. He closed his eyes for a moment, still riding the machine on me in a steady rhythm. When he opened his eyes, he lifted my hand and drew it down to the vibrator.

"Take it from me now."

As soon as I grabbed it and took control, his hand went to his cock and he gave it some overdue fisting while he watched.

I purred and smiled, my heart racing with anticipation. Then I felt his hands beneath my buttocks as he lifted my lower body from the bed, shimmied forward on his knees and rested me into his lap, latching my legs around his neck. The humming vibrator was inches from his face. He slicked his fingers around it and smoothed the excess lube down and into my cleft.

"Oh yes, please let me feel you there," I encouraged. I was already full with my vibrator and its twin assault on my nerve endings. The prospect of more had me stimulated beyond belief. I didn't even know if I could cope; it was sheer lust that was driving me to ask for more.

"Don't worry, I'm coming, I'm coming." His eyes narrowed as he guided his cock between my buttocks.

When I felt the head nudging up against my anus, my sphincter muscle clutched. He pulled my buttocks further apart. I was open, exposed completely, and there was absolutely nothing I could do about it. He began to maneuver his cock into my secret passage, slowly, inexorably slowly, easing me open. Total submission rode over me, bending me to its will, freeing my spirit to its every pleasure. I almost dropped the vibrator.

Edward pushed his cock home. A hot plume of sensation burst up through my pelvis and spine. I rolled my head on the pillow, moaning with inescapable pleasure.

I was full, completely full and more. I was pushed to the limits to accommodate the second intrusion. I was possessed and controlled, impaled on his cock and all too aware of the vibrator, the two rods separated only by a sheath of skin so delicate that each frisson of movement sent shock waves through my entire body, leaving it shuddering and weak. Complete fullness, right into the depths of my soul. I could only roll on each wave of sensation.

"Jesus Christ, that thing is right there." When he experienced the hum of the vibrator against his cock from inside me, his eyes clamped shut. He was shocked. He bit his lip and the muscles stood out like rope on his neck.

"I thought you wanted to watch...Edward?" I gave a manic laugh and with a huge effort, managed to flick the machine up to full throttle.

His eyes snapped open. "Oh, you're bad," he declared, his mouth sliding into a dark but determined smile. He began thrusting hard again, in a steady, urgent rhythm.

I began to come, very quickly, my mouth opening. My entire nether region was awash with waves of bliss.

He swore aloud when he felt me spasm and clutch, his body taut with effort, his hips thrusting ever faster between my buttocks, his eyes avidly watching the display between my spread legs. Panting, his eyes glazed over, his cock was rock hard and at its most swollen as it finally reached its goal. He pulled out as he spilled, and collapsed onto the bed, groaning, his cock still jerking. He made a feeble attempt to dab me dry with the towel then dropped it.

I was weak with sensation, and pulled my knees up to my chest as I tried to regain my physical equilibrium. Catching my breath, I laughed, then said, "Lover, you okay?"

"I think I've gone blind," he murmured, his eyes tightly shut.

I kissed his shoulder and watched as his body slowly relaxed and sank into the bed. After a while, I pulled the covers over him and then spotted his logbook on the bedside cabinet. Reaching over, I lifted it and nudged him with one corner. "You want to make some notes?"

He waved his hand, mumbling incoherently.

I stifled a smile and was about to put the book down, when I changed my mind and flicked it open. Underneath the header he'd written with today's date, I wrote:

Approach with caution. Some parties may be rendered totally incapable of speech or the ability to record data, due to the unexpectedly high levels of acute stimulation triggered by this experiment.

TROPHY WIFE

Kate Dominic

I didn't know where my happy little housewife got the idea that having sex in the garden would make her tomatoes grow better, but I was hooked. There was nothing better than coming home from a long day at the office to find Sharon lounging in the shade of the backyard weeping willow, her skirt hiked to her waist as she fingered her pussy with one hand and held her Palm Pilot in the other, reading one of those damn historical romance novels she was addicted to. She insisted on e-books, so she could electronically change the heroes to butch heroines. It made for some real mind-fuck stories.

Sharon was a femme to the core. She was totally into what she considered the stereotypical happy homemaker look: designer dresses for her fleshy, "voluptuous womanly curves," Italian heels, full makeup every day, and a hairstyle that cost as much to maintain as she used to make in a week when she was "working outside the home," as she so delicately put it, before we met. Sharon got off on being "kept."

That had been the deal-breaker with my last two lovers. After twenty years as an aerospace manager, I could afford to settle down with someone whose priority in life was her relationship with me. I wanted a fucking trophy wife. I didn't give a damn how she spent her time when I wasn't there. But when I walked in the door at night, I expected to come into a clean, comfortable home, to have dinner on the table or reservations made, and to have her undivided attention, as I was willing to give her mine.

Given the reactions of the potential partners I'd met in the interim, I'd listed my relationship expectations up front and clearly with Sharon. I also bluntly told her I expected her to like her career as a housewife. I was willing to pay for maids and a cook and a new car every two years, even spas and jewelry and gardeners, as well as give her a generous allowance for clothing and whatever the hell else she wanted. But I'd done my time with sulking princesses who, as soon as I'd made them financially secure, did a 180 from sultry sweetheart to resentful bitch lusting after unfulfilled career aspirations. When I was home, dammit, I expected my wife to be there!

Sharon didn't want a career or a gardener, though she was okay with the rest. What she wanted more than anything was to live out the fantasies she read about—or rather, her interpretations of them. Those currently ran to being licked and fucked in the shade of the weeping willow that graced the center of our exquisitely landscaped backyard. An eight-foot stone privacy fence surrounded the yard. An herb and vegetable garden, entirely her doing, ran adjacent to the "lounge area" she'd created under the tree, complete with benches large enough to stretch out on.

Sharon loved waiting for me under that tree. She didn't give a tinker's damn that I was in a Milanese designer suit when she grabbed my tie and pulled me down to kneel in front of her hiked-up skirt.

"I'll take your pants to the cleaners tomorrow, baby," she purred, brushing her pussy-scented fingers over my lips. She trailed her hands down my body, then onto her thighs, where her skirt rested against her garter belt. Her soft creamy flesh was framed by blue satin garters and the tops of her suntan-colored stockings. Even though she sunbathed nude, she wore SPF60 sunblock to keep the contrast between her hose and the milky white skin she loved reading about in those damn books. One of her hottest fantasies was of herself as a rich, eighteenth-century aristocrat's woman, which of course meant she would have kept her skin covered by bonnets and would have carried a parasol whenever she went out the door—always with a perfectly butch escort, of course.

Sharon said her favorite fantasy escort was a twentyfirst-century aerospace engineering manager. Me. Damn, that woman was good for my ego! I smiled as I knelt in the grass and put my hands firmly on my lover's widespread creamy thighs. Sharon's neatly trimmed pubes curled around the glistening pink folds of her labia. She especially loved seeing the contrast of my light brown hands against her bare thighs. Mama always told me I was Heinz 57, with just enough Cherokee to get a tan walking across the backyard. Our differences were a big turn-on for Sharon. She leaned back on the gazebo bench and stretched like a cat.

Two pussies make a garden twice as fertile. I read it in a book. Her grin was wicked, modeled after the smiles of the heroines in the stories she read. She practiced her wicked look in her vanity mirror while I watched from the bed. She said she had to pay particular attention to getting the look right when we first started playing one of her fantasies, because her concentration went all to hell when her pussy got humming. She wanted the image of her as a perfect lady completely set in my mind right from the start, so I'd keep thinking of her that way when she was yelling and bucking with complete abandon under my lips or hands or the big blue silicone cock she loved so well.

Sharon never quite got the "69 is always fine" version of woman-woman sex. She was fine with jerking off my clit. When I straddled her face, she sucked the hood back and forth over the nub beneath until I spurted pussy juice down her chin. But her idea of a really hot night always culminated in my fucking her with the biggest dildo I could fit in my Texas two-strap harness—in every hole the damn thing would fit in. She'd insisted we test-drive more vibrators than I could count, until she was certain the butterfly vibe slipped inside the harness between my cock and my clit could make me come, damn near every time.

Sharon was so *Feminist Mystique* un-P.C. she made our friends scream. That was part of her appeal to me. She honest to god really did get off on being a prissy kept woman. And she made it plain to everyone, especially me, that no matter what, being my woman was the highest priority in her life. It made me so hot for her, my mouth aimed for her pussy like a magnet. I had no doubt the grass stains were never going to come out of my summer linen pants. I didn't give a shit. Tomorrow, when the cleaner told her the pants were a lost cause, I knew Sharon would go to the mall and buy me new ones—in a fashionable style that would make me look even more butch than I already did. I put my hands on her thighs and pressed wide, lowering my face to the honeyed scent of her pussy. She was wearing expensive perfume again, no doubt in the crease at the top of each leg and a tiny drop in the crack of her ass, just above her anus. Her pussy glistened hot and pink. I stuck my tongue in her slit and licked up.

Sharon screamed into her fist, the Palm Pilot waving wildly in her other hand. I moved just enough to grab the fragile electronic device and set it gently on the grass. She'd shattered two already that summer, when they went flying from her hand onto the bench. I didn't mind the expense of replacing them, but Sharon was a bitch supreme while she was reloading and reformatting the genders on her favorite stories. When my hand once more pressed against her garter, I started licking her clit.

"Ooh! Up just a little bit!" Sharon thrust against me, mewling as she buried her hands in my short, spiky hair. "YES!"

She has the sweetest, juiciest pussy I've ever tasted, and she has no inhibitions about sharing her wants or her fantasies with me. As I dutifully licked "right there," she bucked and panted against me.

"I was r-reading a Regency, where the hero, Charles, is a wealthy but miserly naturalist recluse. He wants to spend all his time counting his money and writing about how plants respond to the people around them. He has no interest in a w-wife. He marries only to appease his f-family. Right there! Harder!" She wiggled against me, shivering as I teased the spot I knew was guaranteed to rattle her narration. I loved making her lose her train of thought when she was trying to retain her persona, at least enough to bring me up to speed on her latest story. Unlike her desire for fantasies, I was more into the here and now of a hot, willing pussy that had spent the afternoon getting wetter with every minute she waited for me to get home.

I didn't know if the heroines in the stories masturbated. Sharon would masturbate until her fingers were ready to fall off. But she refused to come until I was there. She said that was something proper ladies just didn't do in her books. I moved my hands further in, spreading her labia wider. The tip of her clit peeked out from under its swollen hood.

"I renamed the hero Charlotte." Sharon's voice was fast and breathy, her fingers gripping my hair. "She just writes under the name Ch-Charles—a la G-G-George El-l-l-l-liott. OOH!"

I flicked the exposed nub until Sharon was shuddering, her breath coming in great, heaving pants as she yanked my hair so hard my head hurt. I slipped my middle finger inside her and pressed up.

"Oh, god, yes! Don't make me come! Not yet!" Slippery juice slid onto my tongue as I slowly rubbed my finger inside her. "I want to come while you're fucking me. Just your finger now. No tongue! Press up hard and rub. Sloooowly. Unh!"

Fortunately, by now I was pretty good at predicting Sharon's responses. My tongue was getting ready to fall off. I leaned back, working my jaw from side to side as I massaged the thickening spot on the front wall of her pussy.

"Did Charlotte learn to properly pleasure her wife—while gaining the scientific and literary acclaim she'd no doubt craved all her life?"

I didn't read the damn books, but I'd learned enough to ask the right questions.

"Yes! Ooh! That feels good!" Sharon lifted her hips as a soft flush spread up her neck. "Charlotte purchased an ebony ph-phallus in London. She f-fucked her w-wife senseless with it, every n-night. In her pussy." She groaned loudly again. "And her b-bottom."

I grinned at my honeypot's none-too-subtle hint. I pulled my finger free, sliding both hands down to lift her bottom cheeks. Sharon grabbed a pillow from under the far side of the bench and lifted her hips. I dutifully slid it under her. When she'd once more relaxed, I rubbed her bottom cheeks together, teasing my thumbs over the sensitive skin at the very top of her thighs. "Did the wife like having her bottom fucked?"

"YES!" Sharon moaned as I moved my thumbs, just enough to stretch the edges of the wrinkled skin surrounding her anus. "She liked it a lot. She even liked having a toy in her b-bottom while Charlotte fucked her."

I had the picture now. I slid my fingers up and down, massaging so that Sharon's anal lips rubbed together. She arched up, gasping.

"I have a t-toy here, in my bag." Her hand shaking wildly, she once more reached under the far side of the bench. She pulled up a brightly colored beach bag. It tilted open as she plunked it on her belly. "The red beads. The string is kind of long. I figured you could count them, like Charlotte counting her money, when you put them in. Start with the littlest ones. There's a bottle of lube in the bag."

The big blue dildo and my favorite harness were in the bag as well, right on the top. I couldn't help laughing out loud. Sharon's dirty little imagination was giving those novel authors a run for their money.

I gave her clit one more long, lingering kiss. I stood up, kicked off my shoes, and shucked my jacket and pants. Then I slipped the butterfly vibrator over my hips, buckled the harness on, and slid the dildo into place. Standing there in just my socks and button-down shirt and tie, with my blue silicone cock jutting up between my legs, I knew I was my sweet little wife's hottest butch dream. I straddled the bench below her hips and sat down. I picked up the lube in my right hand and the long, graduated strand of bright red beads in my left. Right hand for pussy, left for bottom. Sharon insisted I keep things separated that way from the start, so I wouldn't get carried away and forget later. Not that I ever had, but like the characters in her really explicit novels, she still worried. I drizzled lube over the beads. Then I squirted the clear viscous liquid onto her anus. The wrinkled pucker quivered as she jumped.

"That's cold!"

I gave her my most wicked laugh. "Your bottom will soon be heated, wench. As will your exceptionally libidinous feminine hole."

I couldn't do romantic language for shit. I thought it was ridiculous. But for Sharon's sake, I did my best. Hooking the ring at the end of the beads over my left middle finger, I picked up the smallest bead. "Relax your nether sphincter, my love. I am about to invade your delicate bottom passage."

Charlotte's wife may have been startled at her spouse's forward ways, but my sweet, demanding wife knew exactly what she wanted. She smiled her appreciation at my literary attempts, shivering with delight as her anus seemed to reach out, relaxed and trembling, to suck the first bead in.

"Yummy!"

Her anus glistened in a shaft of sunlight that made its way into the gazebo. One by one, I rubbed the gradually larger beads against her trembling anus and slowly pressed them in.

"That feels so good!" She paused, panting, and opened her eyes. "I don't hear the vibrator." Sharon's eyes were surprisingly focused as she looked sternly from my face to my cock and back again. "Is something wrong, honey?"

"Everything's fine, my delightful, corrupted wench." The beads were big enough now that it took some pressure, and a conscious effort to relax on Sharon's part, to get them in. Her eyes glazed as I worked another bead against the tiny circle of her anal gate. "I just want to concentrate on filling your hungry little bottom hole. I'll turn the vibrator on when I start fucking you."

She nodded, her eyes closing as she tipped her head back, visibly relaxing her anal muscles as I increased the pressure. She took in a deep breath, and as she released it, she pressed out with her sphincter. She gasped as the bead slipped in.

"Three more, baby, the biggest ones. Pretend I'm counting my money. These are the biggest gold pieces. I'm counting them slowly, running my fingers over them as I put them in my treasure chest and think of all the prizes they're going to bring me."

As far as I was concerned, those nuggets were going to bring me the greatest fortune in the world—my woman orgasming loudly enough to scare the birds from the fucking trees. It was fortunate we had those eight-foot stone walls. I hoped none of the neighbors were home from work yet, or if they were, that they had their TVs on loud. I kept up a running commentary on the wonders of the huge golden nuggets I was working up my beloved's luscious ass. The last one took a while. As she was adjusting to it finally being inside her, I massaged her now puffy sphincter. I could feel the beads moving inside her.

"I'm full." Sharon's voice was hoarse and shaky. I leaned over and kissed the creamy flesh above the top of her stocking.

"I know, honey. The gold is all in the vault. Now I'm going to bring out the family jewels."

Okay, so I suck at romance novels. I did the best I could with my pussy throbbing to fuck her.

I slipped the ring from the string of beads off my finger and stood up enough to grab the ring again from behind. I slid it back on over my left middle finger. Then, using just my right hand, I adjusted the harness so the thick blue silicone cock rode low in my crotch, the base and vibrator centered right over my clit. I slathered lube on my cock and placed it against Sharon's pussy lips. I rubbed back and forth, easing the tip between her glistening pink labia, slowly pressing in until the entire head was in her. With one quick movement, I reached up and flicked the vibrator on. Then I put my right thumb against her clit. And I leaned into her.

There is no sound in my world more beautiful than my wife's cry as she completely opens her body to me. I thrust into her, knowing I wasn't going to last long. The vibrator was working on me just the way Sharon had meant it to. But the dark flush rising up her chest and neck and face told me my staying power wasn't going to be an issue. Her whole body stiffened as she lifted her hips and threw back her head.

"One gold nugget," I rasped. Sharon screamed as I pulled it free. "Two…three…" I counted every one of those damn things, though I doubt she heard any but the first. She was coming, bucking and thrashing so hard I was surprised we didn't fall off the fucking bench. And I couldn't have caught her. I could barely support my own weight. I climaxed so hard my juice spurted onto the harness.

I was still catching my breath when the sirens in the distance told me we were going to have hell to pay with the neighbors. My hands shook as I dragged my cell phone from my jacket pocket and speed dialed the police. They were none too pleased at my wife's "hysterical reaction" at finding a snake in the garden. But by the time the patrol actually made it through the gate and up the driveway, I was dressed and Sharon was once more demurely holding her Palm Pilot and the beach bag in one hand, gripping my fingers with the other. I assured the officers I'd call an exterminator in the morning. They nodded and went on their way. Sharon giggled and led me into the house.

"I've had enough of those damn books!" I growled, pulling my jacket off and tossing it over a chair. I'd been hungry when I left work. Now I was ravenous, though I was more than will-ing to have traded a tryst in the garden for dinner on the table. I froze with my tie half over my head. I smelled—lasagna?

Sharon batted her eyes and marched into the kitchen. "If you can live with microwaved garlic bread, dinner will be ready in ten minutes. That should be enough time for you to change into something more comfortable and to let the wine breathe." She looked coyly back over her shoulder, smiling innocently as she pulled her apron on. "By the way, dear, all the vegetables we're having, including the tomatoes for the red sauce, are from the garden. Thank you for doing your part to ensure the vitality of this season's harvest."

Speechless. The woman left me fucking speechless! I let her shoo me toward the bedroom, where I had enough time to change without hurrying and get ready for what I had no doubt was going to be a magnificent meal. I'll buy the woman all the damn Palm Pilots and e-books she wants to live out her fantasies and consider it money well spent. She makes my dreams come true, better than I'd ever imagined possible.

NATALIE

Michael Hemmingson

I was at Barry's place; we were kicking back and watching some Hong Kong action movies he'd ordered over the Internet. His phone rang. "Yeah, yeah, sure, okay," Barry said and put the phone down. "Natalie's coming over," he said.

I was very interested.

"Oh really," I said.

"Really," he said, and yawned.

I'd wanted to fuck Natalie for several months now. But she always eluded the right time and the right moves. She said she had a boyfriend, but the boyfriend was hardly ever around...he was a freelance roadie and there were always bands that needed him to go on the road and keep their instruments in tune and the tubes up-to-date in the amplifiers, among the other things roadies did.

"She sounds whacked," Barry said.

"Good," I said.

"She drives me up the wall sometimes," he said.

"She needs to get rid of that boyfriend," I said.

"Or he needs to get rid of her," Barry said.

Natalie arrived fifteen minutes later. She was sweaty, smelled like tequila. "Brisk walk," she said, giggling, giving us both a hug and a kiss on the cheek.

"Nice outfit, Natalie," I said.

She was wearing a white cotton tank top and tight white shorts with the word LOOK on her ass. Her ass was hanging out of the shorts. She wasn't wearing a bra, and the cotton top was see-through, especially with that film of sweat....

I imagined Natalie walking the seven blocks from her apartment, that ass swaying, the sweat forming on her skin...and cars honking at her. "Cars always honk at me," she'd said more than once.

"What?" she said.

"I like your jogging gear," I said.

"You like?" she said. "I *bet* you do," she said, looking over her shoulder and smiling at me.

"Oh, I do," said I.

"*Pervert,*" said she.

"And what's so perverted about looking?"

"*Every*thing," she said, walking away, going: "Barry, what do you got to drink around here?"

"There's that bottle of Chivas you left last time," Barry said. "Yum."

"You want to drink more?" he said.

"Glug-glug," Natalie said, holding her head up, mouth open, and pointing a thumb down.

"You're drunk already," Barry said.

"I had a few," she said. "Hey, I'm young, I can drink gallons," she said.

She was twenty-five. Barry was thirty. I was thirty-three.

She made us all a drink.

"Party away, boys," she said. "Hey, what were you two doing? Watching pornos and jerking off?"

"Kung fu movies," Barry said.

Natalie rolled her eyes. "You and your funny movies, kid."

Somehow we wound up in Barry's bedroom. Natalie finished her drink and was lying on the bed, on her stomach. I was sitting next to her, thinking about the right kind of move to make on the girl. Barry stood, looking annoyed, playing with his drink.

"I must be crazy," Natalie said.

"Yes," Barry said, "you are."

"I *must be crazy*," she said, "being here with you two like this. As far as I know, you both might kill me."

"Funny," Barry said. "Look at me: ha ha."

"Ha?"

"Ha."

He seemed uncomfortable.

Natalie turned her head to look at me and said, "Maybe just you. *You*, you might just slice up my flesh and filet me."

"You'd like that," Barry said, "I think."

"You know, I might," she said.

"Filet your ass?" I said, and gave her ass a soft smack.

"Mmm," Natalie went, wiggling her butt.

I smacked it again.

"*Oh*," she said, "you're bad. Will you filet me now?"

"I wouldn't filet this ass," I said. "I'd just fuck it."

"Promises, promises," she mumbled.

I hit her ass, hard.

She wiggled and moaned.

"Bad Natalie," I said.

"I'm very bad," she said. "I need a good spanking."

I smacked both her cheeks a few times.

"I need to get hand to flesh," I said, noticing a few brown pubic hairs sticking out of her shorts.

Natalie lifted herself up as I pulled her shorts down to her ankles . . . one ankle anyway.

"No undies," I said. "Bad Natalie."

"I'm a bad girl, Big Daddy," she said.

I gave her a few more tender slaps, then slid a finger into her cunt.

"Okay, guys," Barry said, "I'll leave you two alone."

"No, stay," Natalie said.

"I'll just be out here," Barry said, stuttering.

I moved a finger into Natalie's asshole.

"You're the bad bad bad boy," she said.

I leaned down and kissed her left cheek, slightly red from my touch.

"Was that a promise or a threat?" she asked me.

"What?"

"That you'd fuck my ass rather than filet it."

"Why don't I do both?"

"I have a boyfriend…."

"Does that matter now?"

"I mean, it's okay if you fuck my ass, but not my pussy."

"Because of your boyfriend?"

"Yeah."

That didn't make sense, but I didn't care. I managed to get a second finger into her asshole.

"You do have a condom, I hope," she said.

"That I have. But hang on. Don't go anywhere."

"I'm right here, Big Daddy."

"Don't call me that," I said.

"Yessir."

I went to the living room. Barry was watching TV. "Hey," I said.

"Hey," he said.

"Do you have any lube?"

"There's some K-Y in the bathroom. Why?"

"Why do you think?"

"Are you really going to fuck her?" Barry asked.

"Finally, yes. Don't you want to?"

"Not really."

"You can go first if you want."

Barry sat up. "Look," he said, "have fun. I'm going for a walk. How long do you need?"

"Don't know."

"I'll be back in an hour," he said, and left.

I returned to the bedroom with the bottle of K-Y. Natalie was still on the bed, a pillow under her hips now. She was playing with her clit.

"I made myself come when you were gone, dude," she said.

I hovered above her, my pants down, the rubber on my cock. I started to apply the K-Y to her.

"Where's Barry?" she asked.

"He left."

"Why?"

"He needed a stroll."

"Does he hate me?"

"No."

"I wish he was here."

"Me too."

I fucked Natalie for fifteen minutes, smacking her little butt-cheeks now and then. "Hit me harder," she said, and I did. By the time I came her rear end was bright red.

I lay down next to her.

"Everything you hoped for?" she said.

I smiled.

"I see how you always look at me," she said.

"It's the way you dress."

"How do I dress? Like a whore?"

"Like you want to get fucked."

"I always want to get fucked," she said. "I just don't get fucked by the right men."

"What do you mean?"

"I wish Barry was here," she said. "He could fuck me next."

"He's not here."

"No, I guess he is not. So you'll have to fuck me again, if you want to."

"I want to," I said.

"You can fuck my pussy this time. My ass is sore, you fucked that too hard and it'll be sore for a week."

She giggled.

I slapped her one across the two cheeks.

She turned over on her back.

"Pussy next," she said. "I want it in the pussy."

"What about your boyfriend?" I asked.

She said, "The hell with him."

I was watching the rest of the interrupted Hong Kong flick when Barry returned, two hours later.

"There you are," I said.

"Where is she?" he said.

"Asleep."

"Passed out, you mean."

I shrugged.

Barry sat down. "So you fucked her?"

"Three times."

"Everything you hoped for?"

I laughed. "She said the same thing."

"Whatever," he said.

"What? Why don't you want her? She wants you to fuck her."

"I know. But I don't want to."

"Why? She's gorgeous, hot, sexy…"

"I work with her, we work at the same goddamn place…."

"So?"

"One," he said, "I don't mess with coworkers. It's bad…"

"So?"

"Two, she has a boyfriend."

"So?"

"Three, she's nuts."

"Ahhh," I said, waving a hand.

"Really," Barry said, "something isn't right in that girl's head."

The next day, Natalie called me while I was jerking off, thinking about her.

"Hey," she said.

"Speak of the devil," I said.

"What's that?"

"How are you?"

"Sober," she said. "Can I come over? We need to talk."

"We can talk on the phone,"

"I want to talk face-to-face," she said, serious.

"Okay," I said.

She knocked on my door half an hour later. She was wearing faded jeans and a purple tank top, again no bra. Hard dark nipples, et cetera. Hair pulled back in a ponytail. Bright lipstick.

"Drink?" I said. "I have vodka…"

"Tempting," she said, "but no."

We sat down on the couch, distance between us.

"Look," she said. "Yesterday."

"Yeah."

"I was really drunk."

"I know."

"You took advantage of me."

"No I didn't."

"Okay, you didn't."

"So," I said.

"So I was upset about something, that's why I got drunk, and I didn't want to be alone. So I called Barry. I came over. And there you were...."

"Regrets?"

"I feel funny."

"Why?"

"I went to Barry's because I wanted Barry to fuck me."

"But not yours truly?" I said.

"Look," she said.

"Should I feel insulted?" I asked.

"Not at all," she said. "I like you."

"Well, that's good," I said with a smile.

"We're friends," she said, "and I don't have many friends, you know."

But my heart felt sad because I knew where she was going.

"You scare me a little," she said. "What I said about you cutting me up and making my meat into filet..."

"Oh come on," I said.

"I'm kidding," she said, but I knew she wasn't.

"It was nice," I said, "being inside you."

"I can see myself being in love with Barry," she said. "But he hates me."

"No he doesn't," I said. "He cares about you."

"Like I was a stray cat."

"The thing with Barry," I started to say.

"He's afraid of women," she said. "He likes his movies better, because movies aren't real."

"No," I said.

"It's because his last girlfriend tore his heart apart," she said.

"Yeah," I said.

"I could mend that heart."

"Do you really want him that much?" I asked.

"It's a fantasy," she said. "Look, my boyfriend can never know what happened between us."

"Okay."

"Well, I don't give a crap. I'm going to break up with him."

"Oh?"

"He's been fucking girls on the road, groupies and shit," she said. "Can you believe that? And I've been so good. Why should I be good? Tell me? Why?"

"You shouldn't," I said.

"No," she said, "I shouldn't."

I pushed the sadness out of my heart and filled the space with a lewd darkness.

"You're bad," I said.

"I am."

"You're a wicked wench," I said. "A naughty slut."

"That's me, boy," she said.

"You should be treated as such."

"I should, shouldn't I?"

"Yes," I said, "and what you're going to do, slut, is lie across my lap right now, and I am going to give you what all bad girls who cheat on their boyfriends get."

"And what's that?"

"The spanking of their lives."

Natalie stood, took off her jeans and panties, and lay across my lap.

"You better hit me really hard," she said.

"I will," I said.

Later, as she got dressed, Natalie said, "This can never happen again, okay?"

"Okay," I said.

"Oh, my ass is going to be so black and blue tomorrow," she said.

"I hope so," I said.

"This is a one-time thing, okay?" she said, looking at the wall.

I nodded; after she left the sadness returned.

Three days later, she called before midnight.

"Sorry," she said. "Asleep?"

"I'm awake."

"I didn't know who to call."

"What's wrong?"

"Nothing's wrong."

"You're calling."

"I wanted to hear your voice," she said.

"I like the sound of your voice, too," I said.

"I broke up with my boyfriend," she said.

I wanted to say *good.*

"He didn't care," she said.

"Where are you?" I asked. I could hear the sound of cars.

"He doesn't know me," Natalie said. "He never whacked my ass like you do. I don't think Barry would either."

"Where are you?"

"A pay phone, three blocks away."

"What are you doing?"

"Can I come over?"

"Of course," I said.

"Will you bend me over and spank me hard?" she said. "Will you tell me how much I'm a very bad, naughty little girl?"

"Of course," I said, "and then some."

"And this time, after you pound my ass raw," she said very softly, "I want you to make love to me."

SOMETHING DIRTY

Erica Dumas

The first time I saw him, I wanted him to fuck me in the ass. You may think I'm a horrible slut for confessing such a thing, but isn't that the point of books like these?

I didn't tell him what I wanted—not in so many words. I never told him that as I stood behind the bar mixing daiquiris and gin-and-tonics, I kept glancing over to him and thinking, *That's it. That's what I want.* I never thought it would become real. I never thought it would actually happen, so I was free to make up a scenario to pass the time. I concocted an elaborate fantasy about him as I mixed, so elaborate that I couldn't get it out of my head. I thought that's all it would ever be—a fantasy. Fantasies are safe. That's why my fantasies go so fucking wild most of the time. Wild, and risky, and—there's no getting around it—dirty. Filthy. Hot.

I don't know for sure why I picked him, but there was just something different about him. The clientele at Amistoso's was the most well-dressed, most affluent, rudest bunch of yuppies you ever saw. Him? There was something dirty about him. I don't mean physically dirty—when he handed me a twenty-dollar bill to pay for his drink, his death's-head-adorned fingers grazed mine and I took note of his trimmed, clean fingernails, something that gave me goose bumps in a way it wouldn't have if he hadn't also been wearing a black goatee, a bandanna, and a Harley-Davidson T-shirt. And in a way it probably wouldn't have if I hadn't noticed his tight leather pants, his high boots, his wide belt, and that impossible swagger.

Oh, I'm not stupid—I know who comes to Amistoso's, and I know who rides Harleys nowadays. He wasn't your classic Hell's Angel, which in any event would have probably scared me off and prevented me from ever making a come-on. He was a computer programmer, probably, or an advertising executive, maybe even a doctor. On Monday he would put on a pin-striped suit or a white coat or a Holy Grail T-shirt and fit right in with the rest of his yuppie pals at work, making enough money that he just had to spend it on a Harley. The friends he was hanging out with were similar weekend-biker yuppies, but they didn't take it as far as he did. I guess that's why he was the one I picked. That, and those impossibly blue eyes.

If I'd worked in a real biker bar, he would have been one of the clean ones. But here, at Amistoso's, he was dirty. Filthy. And the way he looked at my tits when I handed him an Anchor Steam told me I hadn't misread him. I smiled and flirted, which I never do with the stuck-up Polo-shirt-wearing yuppies. Who, by the way, are the whole reason I ended up getting exactly what I wanted.

His name was Trey; I found that out after he came to my rescue. A crew of Marina types got dropped off outside in a limousine and came in with a round of elaborate cocktails decorated with drink umbrellas.

I came out from around the bar, all five-two of me, and told the crowd of yuppies they'd need to lose the drinks or leave—we have our liquor license to think about.

"I don't see what's the fucking problem," one of the yuppies slurred drunkenly, and took a step toward me, then paused to sip his drink.

He probably jumped the gun, you know, and with anyone else it really would have pissed me off. But before the yuppie scum could take his second step, Trey was between me and him, saying, "You've been asked to leave."

All six-two, maybe six-three of him, hands at his sides, not a hint of a threat anywhere but in his voice.

Which is how I found out his name was Trey. The yuppies left, I introduced myself, felt a shiver go through me as I felt his firm handshake; imagined that firm grasp spinning me around and shoving me against the bar, pulling down my stretch jeans and entering me in the filthiest way a knight in shining armor could. His name was Trey. I wanted Trey to fuck me in the ass.

Trey stuck around after his friends had all cleared out. It was after last call, and the bar was mostly empty. I was going to have to clear it out in a minute. He just kept sitting in the corner trying to look like he wasn't watching me. *My very own stalker*, I thought, but that only made the fantasy more intense. I kept running over it in the back of my mind, the filthy thoughts I had of him. He had me over his bike. He had my jeans down around my ankles. He had his cock in my ass.

I was wiping down the tables when he got up and walked over to me.

"Listen, I want to apologize for making a scene with those guys earlier."

I laughed. "You didn't make a scene," I told him. "They did."

He shrugged. "Well, that's good to hear. Listen, I feel bad anyway. I'd offer to buy you a drink, but..."

My heart was pounding; I could see the way he was looking at me, and I only hoped he hadn't seen the way I was looking at him.

"I'll have a drink with you," I said. I glanced around. "Not here, though. I'm sick of this place."

He smiled back at me, his teeth white and capped like a lawyer/doctor/executive's teeth should be. "It's after last call," he said.

I couldn't make eye contact. I just bent over and rubbed down the tables.

"I know a place," I said. "Open all night."

"Is that right?" he said.

"Sure. You okay to drive?"

"Don't you remember what you served me?"

Of course I did—mineral water for the last three rounds, after a number of Anchor Steams. Not very tough of him—but at that point, nothing could dispel the image I had of him. Behind me. Shoving my jeans down. Bending me over his bike.

"I've even got an extra helmet," he said.

I shrugged. "Just let me finish up here."

"Deal," he said, and went back to his seat.

The place cleared without any nasty surprises. I had to serve him up a couple more mineral waters while I counted out the till. But he seemed more than willing to wait. He even took out the trash for me, using the opportunity to have a smoke.

I packed what I needed in the pocket of my waist-length leather jacket, scarcely believing I was doing it. I could always back out, I told myself. I was sure Trey would be a gentleman.

I locked the door behind us and he led me to his bike; I hadn't expected my knees to go all weak like that. There it was—huge and shiny, new, dangerous. It was all I could do not to just bend over it and get what I wanted right then and there.

But I managed to hold off—because I could tell from the way he helped me on with my helmet that I was going to get what I wanted. Exactly the way I wanted it.

He started the bike up, and its low rumble sent a surge through me. He kicked off the stand and I mounted behind him. Fuck, I could feel the rumble through my jeans. When he pulled out onto the street and opened it up, I could have come right there.

"Where are we going?" he shouted.

"Head up Market Street," I told him. "Turn left when I tell you."

So he did, twisting the throttle, beating the speed limit by a good twenty miles an hour. I could feel the throb of the bike going deep into me. Fuck, I couldn't believe I was really going to do it.

He careened around the curves, took the left when I told him, followed my hand gestures for another left, then a right. As we rode, I hugged myself to him, not even aware at first that I was letting my hand drift between his legs. Eventually I discovered he was hard. I splayed my fingers around his cock and felt the rhythm of the bike coursing through me.

"Right here," I told him. He pulled over.

"We're having a drink in the parking lot?"

I got down off the bike. The little lot was marked NO PARK-ING, but I knew the cops never came here. It overlooked the north side of the city, a view more stunning as any tourist could imagine.

I got my helmet off and slid the fifth of vodka out of my jacket pocket. He smiled at me as his helmet came off, but he didn't smile for long.

My lips met his and I tasted beer and cigarettes. He got off the bike and pulled me close, his body hot against me.

"Put it on the center stand," I whispered.

He did, making a grunt as he bounced and lifted the enormous bike. I was down on my knees before he'd turned around.

They were high-quality leathers—and new; the smell intoxicated me as I lowered the zipper. He leaned against the bike as I took his cock into my mouth; he was everything a six-two, maybe six-three man should be. I swallowed as much of him as I could, came up for a little bit of air, and handed him the vodka, looking up at him with his cock still in my mouth.

"This your way of saying thank you?" he said, accepting the vodka and cracking it open.

I shook my head. This was my way of saying "fuck me," but I didn't want to waste time telling him that. Instead I tucked my head to the side so I could lick him all the way from his balls to his head, since there was no way I was going to fit him all in my mouth. Then I took as much of him as I could again, feeling his cockhead nuzzle against the back of my throat, and listened to him moan, low and rumbling and even sexier than the Harley.

He drank from the bottle and met my eyes as I bobbed up and down on his cock.

"You don't waste time, do you?"

I felt a faint flush of shame—Christ, was I really doing this? I didn't even have drunkenness to blame for it, the way most girls leaving a bar with a strange biker would have. But I didn't need an excuse, because I wanted him more than anything, and I wanted him in the way I'd been fantasizing about ever since he walked in the door.

I stood slowly, my mouth still watering from his cock, and wrapped myself around him.

"Anything you want," I whispered into his ear. "Take anything you want from me, Trey."

Anything you want. That's shorthand—for most guys. I had said it enough times before, with predictable results, to know exactly what it meant. There's one thing most guys want, and when you offer it, you don't usually have to offer it twice.

My voice was shaking as I said it—I only hoped he'd take the hint. He didn't, but that only proved he was a gentleman.

At first, though, it didn't matter, because I was so hot for him I lost myself in the hunger. I draped myself over his bike, reaching for my belt as I smelled the lingering gas fumes. I pulled my stretch jeans and thong down to my upper thighs, and he took them the rest of the way down. I put my hands in front of me and gripped the still-warm pipes as I bent over the Harley.

I could only spread my legs a little bit, but it was enough to give him access. He reached under me and discovered what I'd been thinking about all night—or at least that I'd been thinking of him. I was molten. He gave me two fingers and I moaned. He stroked my clit and I snuggled back against him, begging for what I wanted.

His cock was still moist with my spit. I was so wet even his sizeable cock went in without hesitation, but like I said—it was sizeable, impossibly so. I groaned as he entered me, stretching me so that I gasped. It felt tight—even as wet as I was, as bad as I wanted it, this position with my legs only slightly parted made me too snug to comfortably accommodate him.

He could tell it was too tight, and pulled out. Ever the gentleman.

I managed to squirm my booted right foot out of my stretch jeans and spread my legs, pushing myself up onto the Harley so that my feet left the ground.

This time he penetrated me in one smooth thrust, all the way—or as deep as I could take it. I groaned and squirmed there, impaled, suspended over the Harley. It was easy, now, my legs spread wide and my feet propped on the exhaust pipes. I'd lost my jeans from around my left ankle somewhere; now I was naked from the waist down except for my calf-high boots. He began to fuck me as I gripped the Harley, steadying myself. He had me, though—hands firmly gripped to my sides so that I wouldn't slide away, so that I wouldn't upset the bike and hurt myself or him. He knew how to do this. He had done it before.

His thrusts grew in speed, and I heard myself moaning, "Anything you want, Trey—anything," desperately hoping that he would take me that way, the way I'd been dreaming of for hours. He reached his hand under me and touched my clit, working it firmly as he fucked me. I lost myself in the sensations, suspended in midair over a big brawny motorcycle, being fucked by a stranger in the open night air.

Even so, when I came it was unexpected. It shouldn't have surprised me—I'd been fantasizing about this moment all night. Well, not this moment, but what was to come next. I shook the bike wildly as I thrust against him. I surged onto his cock, and Trey had to steady me to keep me from knocking us over.

Trey was letting me recover; I could feel from the way his thrusts slowed. But I didn't want to recover. I wanted him to take me.

I had to bend my arm uncomfortably to get it into the tiny slash pocket of my waist-length jacket. When Trey saw me struggling with it, he tugged my hand out of the way and reached in with two fingers.

They came out holding a lube packet, five milliliters of heaven. Thank god for free samples.

I looked at him over my shoulder, feeling the sweat run into my eyes as his sweat trickled down the backs of my legs. Our eyes locked, and I knew that he knew.

His cock came out of me smoothly. I climbed more firmly onto the bike, spreading wide, hoping it would go back into me just as smoothly.

I was about to get it. Six hours from fantasy to fulfillment. Trey was down on his knees behind me, and I felt his tongue snaking its way between my cheeks. I moaned wildly as he worked in circles around the entrance. I would have reached back and spread myself for him, letting him know that I was asking for it—if I hadn't been clinging precariously to a Harley. As it was, I had to beg him with my moans.

He got the picture—I wanted more. I wanted him inside my ass. He opened the lube packet with his teeth, drizzled it over his cock. I felt his thick head nudging its way into my entrance. I would have said, "Yes!" but I was too overwhelmed.

Besides, he didn't need any more encouragement. He'd gotten the picture, and he was going to take me.

He worked his slick cockhead up to my asshole, going slow. I wanted him to go fast; I had wanted him to go fast all night. But when he held me down against the bike and pushed in, it was plenty fast.

I gasped as he penetrated me; he took a moment to let my snug entrance acclimate to his cock, then slid in gradually until I was moaning. He put it all the way in. I wriggled back against him, reaching one hand down to feel where it stretched me.

"All right?" he asked.

"More than all right," I grunted. "Do it hard."

His hips began to pump, and I moaned "Jesus!" and put my hands down so I could hold on to the bike. He started to fuck me faster, his big hands gripping my waist. I could feel it filling me up, rubbing against my G-spot. I was going to come again—already. Barely half a minute into being fucked. My moans echoed in the around the empty lot and off into the distance. He picked up speed.

I came on his cock, my rear hole clenching tight around his shaft as he fucked me. He thrust into me again, again, again—his movements getting jerky as he got closer.

"Is it all right?" he gasped.

"Yes," I whimpered back, knowing exactly what he meant—exactly what I wanted, his come inside me. He groaned and thrust in deep, and I could feel the pulsing spasms of his cock as he emptied himself into me. His strokes got slick as his come burst inside me. He gave three more short, jerky thrusts—and then he was finished.

He tugged his cock out of me, and I felt a hungry absence where a moment before he had filled me up. He helped me down from where I lay stretched over the bike and kissed me, not even caring that his cock had been in my mouth just a little while before. His hand gripped one of my asscheeks possessively, as if he owned it. I rubbed my face against his neck and breathed in his scent.

My jeans were filthy; they'd landed in a puddle. The zebra-striped thong wasn't even salvageable; I left it in the bushes and squirmed into my stretch jeans without underwear. I could feel myself leaking as I climbed onto the rumbling Harley. The vibrations of the bike made my wide-opened back door tingle with sensation as I wrapped my arms around his waist and held on for the ride home. If my apartment had been ten minutes further, I probably could have come.

That was last night. Fifteen hours ago. He dropped me at my front door, and I didn't even invite him in. I probably couldn't have managed much more, anyway.

It's even worse, tonight, at the start of the evening, only an hour into my shift. The fantasy, I mean. It's more vivid than ever, because it really happened, and I've relived it already a dozen times since I started work. I slipped into the bathroom a minute ago, to feel how wet I was. I was drenched, and I can still feel the absence where his cock filled me up last night.

I keep thinking about it—how he bent me over, pulled down my jeans, fucked me that way. That dirty, filthy way. He'd done something dirty to me, something so dirty I'd never again be clean—thank god.

I can't get the feel of it out of my head as I blend margaritas and mix cosmopolitans. I can't get the ache to go away.

But it's the rumbling that really sends a shiver through my body, making my pussy wet, making my ass hungry. The rumbling as I hear a Harley outside, a single Harley, so loud it makes the windows shake.

My heart pounds; my breath comes short. Hands shaking, I reach into the cooler and pull out an Anchor Steam.

OFF THE RIM

Ayre Riley

love watching Michael play basketball at the Y. It's the *Hollywood* Y—yes, act impressed now. This is a place for guys who are too cool to sign up for the expensive look-at-me gym. That doesn't mean they don't have the money. It means they're serious about playing rough. They like gyms without too many mirrors and too many posers. They like gyms that have that locker-room smell you remember from high school. You will find no incense burning near the showers here, and there are no fruit smoothies at the snack bar, because there ain't no snack bar.

But the guys on his team are all actors. Or wannabe actors. Or bartenders and waiters so handsome they should be actors. They *could* be posers if they wanted to. They're pretty enough. Michael fits right in, a writer, not an actor, but handsome as all the others on his team. I watch him make his famous three-point shot, and I squeal as the ball bounces off the rim and slips silently into the basket.

Maybe that winning shot is why I have rimming on my mind when we get home.

"I'm sweaty," he grins, pushing me away when I stalk toward him. "Let me shower, baby. Then you can have your way with me."

"I want my way with you *now*," I insist, my hands already pulling his slippery blue shorts down his muscular thighs, tripping him as he tries to kick his battered gray sneakers off first. He's bigger than me, and much, much stronger, but he lets me take charge, because he knows he'll get pleasure that way. I have him on his back on the center of the bed in no time, but he still tries to get me to let him bathe.

"Come on, kid," he says, and the fine lines around his green eyes crinkle at me. God, is he gorgeous. "Ever hear about a post-workout shower? I could use a little soap and water first."

"Nah," I shake my head, and my long hair falls free from its loose auburn ponytail. "Can't wait," I murmur. I'm crawling up his long body as he pushes back on the bed. His shoes are off in two quick kicks, and a second after his shorts lay tangled on the floor, but his sweaty shirt still sticks to his chest, and I press my face against it and revel in his scent.

"You don't want me clean?" There's an evil glint in his eyes now as he asks the question. He knows precisely what I want. We've been here before. That doesn't mean he won't make me say it.

"Nah," I say again, pushing at him, butting at him like an animal in my quest to make him turn over. I have his elastic waistband in my hands and I tear his BVDs down his thighs, let him kick them off. I am between the cheeks of his ass before he knows what's happening. Before he can say *no* or *wait* or *stop*. Not that he'd say any those things. But he doesn't even have a chance.

In a second, I am licking in a line up his crack while he lies as still as possible. This isn't something I do all the time, but when I get the urge, I can't stop myself. I am insatiable. I have to taste him, to cleave myself to him, to press my face against this part of his body and devour him. I want to be as close as I possibly can to him, would crawl up inside of him if I could.

He makes no noise at all while I lick up and down, but when I start to slowly circle his asshole with the pointy tip of my tongue, he groans. I know that his fists are clenched tightly at his sides, know that if I were to stop what I'm doing and climb up the bed to get a look at his face, I'd see an expression of half surrender, half pain. His dark green eyes are closed, I'm certain of it. His chiseled jaw is clenched tight. There's a fierce expression on his face. I'm not hurting him, far from it, but I understand that giving up like this causes him some degree of discomfort. Usually, *I'm* the one stripped bare in the center of the bed. I'm the one with my fists clenched tight and my bottom lip bitten nearly to blood. Now, he's starring in the role as the subservient one. *He's* getting eaten, and he never knows precisely how to process this fact.

I don't want him to process anything.

I've been thinking about this moment since I saw the calendar this morning, saw that he was playing at the Y. I've been craving this sensation all day.

I want him to lie there and take it. I want him to lie there and *want* it.

When he groans again, I know that he does.

Now, I spread his cheeks wide apart with my small hands so I can see what I'm doing. The gesture opens him up, exposes him to the air in the room, to my intense gaze, and his breathing goes ragged and rough, like when he's running up the court after the ball, his stride perfect, his body like a machine. I slide my tongue into his asshole, gently at first, and he shudders all over. Then I slide my tongue in again, faster now, in and out. His moans deepen, and I feel the pleasure vibrate through him. I know how much he loves this, and I also know that he will never ask me to do it to him. He waits until I have the need, until I am consumed by the lust of devouring him, and then he lets me have my way.

I am literally fucking him now, fucking him seriously with my tongue, and he has accepted this. I can tell. He's letting go, letting me take him exactly how I need to.

When I realize he's ready for more, I move my mouth away from his body and lick my pointer and middle finger. I overlap them, and then plunge forward, thrusting my fingers inside of him. I think of fucking him with a cock. For an instant, I wish I had one—wish I could strap one on, or mold one out of my own skin to satisfy him. Someday, maybe. Not now. Not yet. Now, I take care of all of his needs with my own body. But I miss his taste, so I bring my mouth back into play, taking turns, licking and thrusting with my tongue, then finger-fucking him until he is crazy from the rhythm of it.

"Oh, Jesus," he groans. "Oh, fuck—"

I do. I fuck him firmly with my tongue, and he starts to buck against the bed. This is my cue to reach under him and cup his balls, then gradually start to jack his cock. I move my fist in perfect time. His cock is dripping, and I use his own lubrication to work my hand faster. My fist is his lover, my tongue is his fantasy. And like a good player, I never let my teammate down. I move my hand exactly in rhythm with my tongue, and I feel him tense and relax, tense tighter and hold, waiting for the explosion of release, waiting for utter surrender; waiting for the shot to hit the rim, reverberate for several long seconds, and slide silently home.

MAKING
WHOOPIE

Marilyn Jaye Lewis

Evan's oceanfront home in Maui was a spectacular monument to modernism. Constructed in jutting geometric angles and utilizing windows of a massive height, it created the illusion—at the back of the house, anyway—of a structure having no walls at all. Evan could lie alone in the evening, on the great expanse of his austerely appointed king-sized bed, contemplate the unob-structed panorama of sunset and crashing waves outside his bed-room window—eleven-foot sheets of sheer uninterrupted glass—and feel as if he were the only living soul in God's universe.

The truth, however, was quite different. Evan couldn't remember the last time he'd been alone. Not only was Cheng, Evan's cook, in the kitchen directly underneath him preparing dinner, but Evan was currently one of the more famous movie stars in the English-speaking world. Beyond the tall privacy wall that guarded the street side of his modern edifice of concrete and glass, there was a never-ending parade of people—most of them curious strangers with cameras. Strangers by the thousands,

it sometimes seemed to Evan, even in the relative remoteness of
Maui. And within the hour, Dorianne and all her luggage would
be arriving from Honolulu, en route from Los Angeles. Evan
might never be completely alone again.

This was it. This was the final hour. If everything proceeded
as planned, Evan and Dorianne would legally be husband and
wife before the night was over. It was going to be a small and
private ceremony: the bride, the groom and the judge, with Cheng
and the judge's wife serving as witnesses. How they had managed
to keep the news of the impending marriage out of the papers
was still a mystery to Evan, but it was further proof that when he
truly desired to keep a thing private, it could be accomplished.

At the age of forty, Evan Crane, who had been in the public
eye since his midtwenties, had quite an impressive list of things
he had managed to keep private—most notably, a long string of
homosexual liaisons.

Dorianne was well aware of most of them, and in fact had
even participated in a three-way with Evan and one of his male
lovers once, back in Los Angeles. The result of the tryst had bor-
dered on being disastrous, though. It had started out promis-
ingly enough. Evan had been impressed, even a little taken
aback, by Dorianne's capacity for lust, her willingness to be
accommodating with her mouth and to surrender her holes to
the repeated poundings of both men. But ultimately, Dorianne
had been left sleeping alone in the master bedroom, while Evan
and Giovanni had slipped downstairs to fuck without her, like
voracious animals, on the living room couch.

"You don't have to deny it, Evan," Dorianne had spat the following morning when Giovanni had left. "You think I couldn't
hear you? All that carrying on?"

"Why are you getting so angry?" Evan had shouted. "I
warned you Giovanni was insatiable. You knew it was likely to

get complicated. I don't even understand why you agreed to do it in the first place."

"Maybe it turned me on to try two men at once, Evan, did you ever consider that? That I might have my own fantasies? Or maybe I did it because I'm trying to understand you better—the things you want. Would that be so horrible, if I cared about you?"

It was at that moment that Evan first realized he might be in love with Dorianne, that she might be "the one." She was fiery and not afraid to speak her mind. She didn't kowtow to Evan like everybody else did. He was turned on by her passion, by how she stood her ground, and most of all by how she seemed to genuinely care. Over the years, Evan had learned some hard lessons about how to keep his ego in check and resist the constant temptation to have sex with every woman who threw herself at him. (Or every man, for that matter.) As much as he might have used his fame to score pussy and ass whenever he'd wanted it, he had just as frequently been used by the people he'd fucked. They objectified him and never seemed to care who he really was under all that fame as long as they could say they'd fucked him.

Dorianne was not a sycophant; Evan had recognized this from the start. Still, during the first year he'd dated her, there was always another lover hidden somewhere. Perhaps right in Los Angeles, or sometimes a continent away. He went through a whole pack of meaningless sex partners before coming to the obvious conclusion that he could better protect his own interests by resisting temptation.

Until recently, even Cheng's position as cook had been filled by a much younger man, James, a man whose talents hadn't confined him to the kitchen. Evan stared out at the vivid sunset and thought about James. What a little slice of heaven he'd been in the beginning, before he'd gotten envious of Dorianne, before he'd gotten contentious and belligerent, acting more like a spurned lover than an employee; then, Evan had been forced to let him go. Evan felt his cock twitching beneath his linen trousers at the mere thought of James, though. Not that James had been a better lover than Dorianne, but he had been incredibly convenient. James had never seemed to aspire to anything higher in life than to suck or be fucked. Evan could summon James day or night and be obliged with a blow job on the spot. James seemed happy to be on his knees—on the kitchen tiles, on the bathroom marble, or out on the concrete lanai in the moonlight, as the furious waves crashed against the black lava rocks beneath them. James had an eager mouth and he swallowed without flinching. His devotion to servitude made him irresistible in any position. It hadn't been unusual for Evan to disturb James in the middle of the night, to wake him from a sound sleep, and James would never complain. He'd obligingly turn over and pull down the blankets. He was always naked under those blankets, Evan remembered; always ready. And he didn't require any of that delaying foreplay as long as Evan was sufficiently lubed.

Evan's hardening cock began to ache with the visceral memory of how effortless and uncomplicated it had been to fuck James. James would part his legs, raise his rump slightly, and let Evan mount him. His asshole always seemed responsive, too; relaxed—ready for Evan's substantial tool as it ploughed into him. James never protested. He'd lie quietly on his stomach and whimper a little, but give Evan complete access to that tight, hot passageway until Evan's cock had had its fill of fucking it.

He glanced at the bedside clock now; trying to gauge if he had enough time to jerk off before Dorianne arrived from Honolulu. Evan loved thinking about fucking James's ass and jerking off. It wasn't that Dorianne didn't turn him on, or that she refused to take it up the ass. In fact, when she was in the right mood, Dorianne could get just as filthy and take it just as hard as any man Evan had ever fucked. But getting her in the right mood for anal sex was sometimes a chore; she was a little intimidated by it. Evan was almost *too* endowed; his equipment, he knew, was huge. It was part of why he'd lasted so long in Hollywood.

Assuming she arrived on time, Evan figured he had just over forty-five minutes to get where he wanted to go. That was plenty of time. He pulled open the nightstand drawer for a squirt of his favorite lube and the one, lone filmy stocking Dorianne had left behind last time caught his eye. She was definitely worth her weight in gold, that woman. She had such a nasty imagination.

Evan retrieved the stocking from the drawer and studied it, remembering how she had tormented him, using it to tie his hands behind him and then bending him over the bamboo trunk at the foot of the bed. She'd alternated licking his balls that night with an incredibly well-paced rim job. She had driven his cock crazy by practically ignoring it. Every once in a while she'd suck the swollen head of his shaft into her mouth, or swipe a dribble of precum from his piss slit with the tip of her tongue, but other than that she'd focused on the rimming. Her delicate hands kept the taut globes of his ass spread wide so that his puckered hole was at the mercy of her mouth.

Evan knew there'd been no real reason to tie him up for a thing like that. It was something he'd have submitted to willingly, but he liked that she'd pretended he hadn't had any options.

He released his hard cock from inside his trousers, slathered it with the lube and suddenly realized James was no longer on his mind. He was wondering instead what it was going to be like to be married. He knew that it was normal for the flame of passion to fade from most marriages, but he couldn't picture it happening between him and Dorianne. Only the night before he'd been half-crazy with lust for her, calling her at her hotel on Waikiki, waking her, insisting they get off together over the phone. Even though she'd been groggy with sleep, he'd known the words that would get to her, trigger her hormones to flow through her like a river of fire, flooding her gorgeous pussy until she was wide awake and touching herself.

"Remember what it was like," his voice had caressed her through the phone wires, "that first time I took you up to my room, back when I had that house in the hills? Remember that, Dorianne? What a filthy little girl you were. You really surprised me that night. Remember what I made you do?"

"Yes," Dorianne's breathy voice had come back at him in the darkness. "I remember."

"Tell me what you remember."

"You made me pull up my dress and pull down my panties."

"And what else?"

"You made me get down on my knees."

"And then what did I make you do?"

"Unzip your trousers with my teeth and lick your cock."

Evan loved to hear the word *cock* coming out of Dorianne's mouth. She had a way of making the whole notion of a cock seem scary to her, scarier than he knew it could possibly be, but it made her mouth sound vulnerable just the same. "That's right," he'd said. "You did such dirty things with my cock that night, didn't you?"

"Yes."

"Why did you do it, Dorianne? Why were you such a nasty little girl?"

"Because," she'd whispered, "I'm your slut, Evan, you know that. I'm a slave to your cock. I'll do whatever you ask me to do as long as I know I can have that big cock of yours in one of my tight holes."

"Oh yeah? Do I get to choose which tight hole I put it in?"

"Yeah."

"Even your asshole, Dorianne? You're going to take me up your tight ass?"

"Yes."

"All the way up?"

"Yes. Even if makes me sweat."

"If what makes you sweat?"

"Feeling myself stretched open back there—your cock is huge."

They had gone on like that for nearly an hour. Evan hadn't been able to stand the idea of hanging up, of being alone without her in his bed, even for the final night. But eventually she'd insisted that she had to get some sleep, even though he hadn't come yet. "I'm going to be a blushing bride tomorrow, Evan, remember? I'm forty-three years old. I'm going to need all the help I can get."

Evan liked the idea that she was older than he was. It satisfied his occasional fantasy of having an older woman take charge of him. "Okay, Dorianne," he'd conceded, preparing to hang up at last, "I'll let you go this time. But after tomorrow, I'm never letting you go again." Then he'd been alone in the darkness, his fist around his aching cock. Much like he was now—thinking of Dorianne naked, her long legs parted, revealing the closely clipped black hairs that set off the fiery pink flesh of her engorged pussy when she was fully aroused, breathing hard and waiting for him to mount her.

Evan loved the sight of her like that. He knew from experience that she would cry out and clutch at his hair, his back, his ass, when he finally lay down on her, penetrated her and gave it to her hard.

He liked to hear her passionate cries in his ear. Sometimes it sounded as if she were in pain.

His fist slid languorously over the slippery head of his cock as he thought about Dorianne and those cries she made. In his mind, he replayed the night he and Giovanni had both gone at her—it was one of his favorite memories. She'd gotten especially worked up when she was on all fours getting it at both ends at once. Giovanni had had a firm grip on her ass as he'd pounded his uncut meat into Dorianne's vagina. Evan couldn't get enough of watching it. He'd been on his knees in front of her, his erection filling her mouth as she grunted from the force of Giovanni's rhythm. Evan had dug his fingers into Dorianne's hair, grabbing it in fistfuls while he'd fucked her mouth hard. He'd known they were getting rough with her, but she seemed to be wildly into it.

Evan worked his cock more vigorously now, tugging it faster, in time to the visions replaying in his head. He loved to think of Dorianne as a slut, as his own perfect slut, taking whatever he could dole out. He couldn't wait to be with her again; he hadn't slept with her in nearly a week. Tonight he was going to devour her; he was that ravenous for her sex.

They would be married then, he realized. Somewhere in the back of his brain the thought agitated him—what about the men, he wondered? Was she really going to be okay with his occasional men? She had thought it over. She had said she would deal with it somehow. Bisexuality didn't just disappear because a person uttered some marriage vows. They both knew it.

Evan decided to worry about it later. For now, he wanted to continue watching Dorianne get good and fucked in his head. He knew that, for the most part, she had loved it that night with Giovanni—she had loved being filled up, utilized, put through it for hours. Evan thought about her being on the airplane, flying first-class; everything about Dorianne was first-class. He figured no one would ever guess—not the flight attendants, the other passengers, or the driver who was waiting for her at the gate. None of them would ever suspect that she was a woman who would prefer to be naked and on all fours, getting it hard at both ends from two men at once.

Mrs. Dorianne Crane.

Evan turned it over in his mind and thought the name suited her perfectly. He wondered if she was going to keep her own name—he'd never bothered to ask. He'd try to remember to ask her later. He was concentrating now on having her to himself, having her naked and underneath him; his swollen cock pushing into her vagina and feeling it open for him. He was so tired of fucking his own hand. He wanted to feel his chest pressed down against her soft breasts, her legs wrapped around him tightly, her hands grabbing onto his ass and holding him down, grinding against him like she couldn't get enough of his hard cock in her hole....

He was very close to coming; he could feel the pressure in his balls—and then he heard her downstairs. Damn, she was either early or he'd miscalculated.

He swung out of bed and hurried into the bathroom to wash his hands, wipe off his cock and zip it neatly into his trousers. It was probably better this way, he thought. Tonight she would be in his arms and his orgasm would explode into her.

Evan headed down the stairs and soon he could see Dorianne in the kitchen, talking animatedly with Cheng. She was smiling; she was beautiful. *She's definitely first-class,* he told himself again. Evan hoped it would last a lifetime. He was going to give it his best shot.

ANTONIA'S BEAST

Dante Davidson

My best friend, Antonia, is a wisp of a girl, with pale blonde hair as soft as eiderdown and a translucent complexion reminiscent of a Pre-Raphaelite model. Sometimes she wears layered antique slips snagged from secondhand stores on Melrose. Clad in faded rose satin with lace at the collar, she might have just stepped out of a nineteenth-century print, a low flush to her cheeks, a secret half-smile on her lips. Other times, she wears those gauzy, ethereal dresses that are so in right now. Always, she looks like a half-frightened wood nymph, her cherry red hair loose and alluring around her cameo face.

I know that her fashion sense makes it sound as if she's not shy, but bold and forthcoming about both her sexuality and sensuality. This is not the case. She has a beautiful body that she dresses in a seductive manner. But her composure is one that Miss Manners would approve of entirely. She is discreet and charming. She doesn't have a bad word to say about anybody. She blushes whenever anyone stares at her for one beat too long.

I am often guilty of this mild infraction.

Antonia works at a café across the street from my office. She makes dreamy confections behind the counter, piling on whipped cream, chocolate shavings, dashes of cinnamon, and just a touch of amaretto. On my breaks, I come over and sit on one of the high-backed stools, waiting for her to take a moment and serve me, to come out from behind the chrome counter and sit at my side.

My best friend is a demure spirit, and yet within her heart lingers an impish creature who peeks out from time to time. When this fiend takes over, Antonia changes. She becomes bolder. She speaks in a louder voice. She drapes a diaphanous shawl across bare shoulders and teases me with the fringe.

She tells me stories.

"Did you ever hear about Marc?" she asks, innocent sounding, but I know the undercurrent of her tone.

"The musician?" I ask, thinking to myself that the fiend is loose, the imp is out, the beast within Antonia's breast is free for the afternoon.

She nods and sips from my mocha, leaving a sparkly lipstick kiss imprinted on the rim of my cup. The whipped cream makes a moustache on her upper lip and she flicks her tongue out to lick it clean. I find myself teetering on the brink of fainting when she does that, thinking of so many other dirty places she could place that darting, kittenish tongue.

Antonia brings me back. "Yes, the musician. Did I ever tell you about the time with the baby oil?"

The businessman seated at Antonia's right perks up. I can tell that he's stopped reading his newspaper and is paying close attention to our conversation. At times like this, when Antonia's beast roams free and she is ready to share, all eavesdroppers are in for a treat. The change may occur in a bookstore, at a theater before the film starts, in line at the grocery store. I watch the man lean slightly closer to Antonia, and I wait for her to notice, but she doesn't.

"The baby oil?" I ask, widening my eyes, urging her to continue, to thrill me. "No, I don't believe you ever told me about the baby oil."

She takes another sip of my drink. Then she says, "Marcus used to play his guitar all the time. Whenever he wasn't on stage, he pretended he was. It wasn't about practicing, for him. It was about *performing*."

I have clients in the music industry. I nod to show that I understand.

Antonia's story goes like this: Marcus was sitting on their water bed strumming his guitar. In his mind, he was performing for an audience of a thousand beautiful women. In reality, his one beautiful woman, Antonia, was taking a shower. The door was open, and she could hear the faint melody of his songs above the spray of the water. When she emerged, wrapped in a towel, she stood in the doorway and watched him play. Marcus was a particularly appealing performer. He had long black hair that hung straight and glossy down his back. He was thin and looked good in tight leather pants. Colorful tattoos decorated his biceps and his chest. In short, he was perfect Hollywood masturbatory fodder.

When Antonia caught his attention, he looked up at her with a glazed, Rock God expression. She stood there, with the steam from the shower still dispersing behind her, red hair curling from the moisture, face flushed from the heat. She approached with a bottle of baby oil in one hand, and he put down the guitar, as if anticipating that something magic was going to happen. She gave him the bottle, and he took her over his lap and spread the clear oil all over her legs, from her ankles to her thighs. He worked her thoroughly, as if still on stage in his head, as if still in the part of the performer. He played music on her body, using his fingertips, using the full palms of his hands, rubbing, rubbing. Then he moved higher, massaging the cheeks of her ass, and in between them.

Stop the story: the man at the counter is having heart palpitations imagining lovely Antonia on her stomach, ass up, legs spread, her honeyed nectar mingling with that pure, undiluted scent of baby oil. I swallow hard. The man swallows hard. Antonia continues, oblivious.

She tells it like she's telling a bedtime story, in a low lilting voice that has a rhythmic pulse to it: they've never fucked like that.

She hesitates, makes herself continue. They've never had anal sex. He's never tried, and she certainly wouldn't have suggested it. But his fingers slowly start to probe her back door. His pointer and his middle finger push their way inside this tightest of openings. She sighs. She clings to his leg. She lets him continue. He makes circles with his fingertips as he delves further. Antonia's breathing speeds up. She feels as if she's going to pass out. She begs him to stop, but she doesn't mean it.

Marcus is gentle, but persistent. He lubes her up and massages her until she is relaxed and ready. More than ready, dying for it. She is inexperienced and she wants suddenly to be experienced. She moves off his lap and waits while he undoes his faded jeans and pulls them down. He mounts her on their rolling, bucking water bed, moving with the motions, gliding inside her. She buries her head in her arms, her face crimson with a combination of shame and lust. They don't speak, but as he builds up to climax, he strokes her hair and murmurs something under his breath that sounds like one of the lyrics in his songs.

Freeze-frame. The man at Antonia's side wants to know the lyric. I want to know the lyric. He's leaned over so far that he's practically in her lap. She still is unaware of his intrusion.

I don't point it out for fear that she'll stop talking, for fear that Antonia's beast will shift-change back into the wood nymph I am accustomed to.

She squirms on the chair as if the retelling of this memory has excited her in the same way that it's excited her audience. I can't help myself. I ask, "What did he sing?"

She looks at me, her eyes registering me for the first time during her story. She says, "I don't remember," but I can tell that she's lying. She says, "The best part was the way he moved. He always moved as if he were in front of an audience. I don't mean posing, but confident, strong. In control. He made love the same way, he fucked"—Antonia never says *fuck*—"the same way."

And when he took her like that, like an animal, like a Rock God should, the imaginary audience of thousands broke into thunderous applause.

HOW CAN I HELP YOU?

Sage Vivant

Nicholas had teased her about finding the kind of bar in San Francisco that made the city famous; a place where sexual preference was irrelevant, gender was mutable, and public displays of everything short of fornication were common.

They settled for Café du Nord, a hip, slightly run-down establishment furnished and lit by more than enough bordello red. The patrons ranged from shy geeks to outrageous performers but the atmosphere held enough mystery to keep Nicholas and Claree there for several drinks.

The tables varied in size, and each had its own arrangement of (formerly) plush seating. As the couple snuggled in a faded *rouge* Victorian settee, Nicholas whispered into her hair.

"Check out Miss Lonelyhearts over there." He tried to nod in the woman's general direction but since he was embracing Claree from behind, it took her a few minutes to figure out which woman he meant. When she located the subject of his remarks, though, she knew exactly what he referred to and giggled. The blonde with two wispy streaks of blue to frame her pretty but painted face pouted on her perch at the bar. She caught Nicholas and Claree looking at her but instead of turning away, she held the gaze and let her mouth slide into a mischievous grin.

"Oh, now you've done it," Nicholas teased. "She's noticed us."

"I think she's just noticed you."

"Well, in any event, we're about to get a visitation."

The odd but intriguing woman approached. The slow, studied sway of her walk accentuated the cinched bustier's effect on her slim waist and rounded hips. Her tits nestled firmly into the cups of the garment but with every step she took, they jiggled just enough to communicate their preference for freedom. Hollywood would have considered her overweight but Claree knew that Nicholas would find her on the tasty side of luscious. Claree was surprised to note she shared that opinion.

The woman finally arrived after a breathtaking but nearly interminable saunter toward them, raised her eyebrows, and pointed to the remaining space on the settee. There was room for one more body, so Nicholas gestured that she seat herself next to Claree.

Up close, the woman's skin—from décolletage to hairline—had a dewy, delicate quality that contrasted sharply, almost comically, with the heavy kohl of her eye makeup. She was Heidi in Transylvania. Despite the jarring streaks of blue in her hair and the burgundy slash of color at her mouth, there was a disarming sweetness about her. Her age was hard to pinpoint—Claree guessed somewhere in her early twenties.

Nicholas's arms were still wrapped around Claree as she leaned back into his warm chest, which had become decidedly warmer with the arrival of this goth angel. He extended a hand to the woman, probably to elicit words from her but also because he was an outgoing kind of guy.

"Hi, I'm Nicholas and this is Claree."

She smiled, thereby subtracting yet another five years. "Laura. I think you don't live in San Francisco."

They laughed politely, even though the comment irritated Claree. What was Laura trying to say? That they looked like hicks or something?

"No, we're here from Suisun City."

"I could tell because you look too happy."

"Well, we are," Claree agreed, relieved that her assumption about Laura had been wrong.

"I love that. It really turns me on." Laura's big blue eyes—a disconcerting visual echo of the stripes in her hair—widened earnestly. Her breasts heaved slightly and Claree couldn't help but watch them settle back into place when the sigh had passed.

"Do you like big tits?" Laura's head tilted and she awaited a response from either Nicholas or Claree or both.

"Yes," they answered in unison, laughing at their timing.

"I'm glad. I like them too. Yours are nice," she nodded at Claree's formidable pair. Claree blushed, more out of pride than embarrassment. "I have a dildo in my bag. Wouldn't it be fun to use it?"

Claree decided to leave this one up to Nicholas. They'd often talked about a threesome. Well, more of a slave situation, really, and Laura seemed a far cry from a dominatrix, so perhaps this was the opportunity they'd been waiting for.

He turned around to look directly at Claree. The bar's red lights and furnishings gave rich depth to his brown hair and eyes and made his tanned skin appear darker. She read his interest as well as his caution. The angle of his eyebrows told her he needed her encouragement.

"I think we have time, don't we, honey?" Claree asked.

Laura led them to a third-floor walk-up about two blocks away in the Castro neighborhood. Like its owner, the flat spoke of fairy tales, death, sprites, and crucifixes. Turquoise, heart-shaped pillows were strewn below an Edward Gorey print, while a tarantula sat patiently in its terrarium. A Britney Spears compact disc lay on the stereo. Claree imagined Laura's underwear—the days of the week scrawled in blood.

Laura took her time lighting candles. As she moved about the room, she told the couple they could get naked if they wanted to.

"As soon as I'm finished here, I'd really like to fuck you both up the ass," she said, as if announcing what ride she planned to enjoy next at Disneyland.

Nicholas and Claree undressed themselves down to under-clothes. The cool San Francisco night air floated through the room, chilling Claree slightly. She looked over at Nicholas, whose erection was as stiff as her nipples.

"Oh!" Laura exclaimed when she noticed Nicholas's bulge. "Won't you take those off so I can see you?"

Nicholas glanced at Claree, who nodded and grinned. He stepped out of his briefs quickly, revealing all eight glorious inches of compliance.

"And I know you don't want to hide those pretty titties," she smiled at Claree, who instantly unhooked her bra and flung it off happily.

Laura unsnapped her skirt and waited for it to whoosh to the floor at her feet. Then she kicked the garment aside and knelt before Nicholas. She didn't attempt to remove the bustier. With no fanfare but surprising concentration, she swooped down on his cock. He nearly teetered at the sudden intensity of her sucking.

From where Claree stood in tingling awe, the finesse with which Laura made Nicholas's cock disappear and reappear again between her dark lips was uncannily like the method

Claree herself used on him. How did this woman know exactly what he liked? Come to think of it, how did she know they would respond positively to her invitation to anal play?

Nicholas's groans interrupted her musings. As Laura sucked, he thrust himself in and out of her mouth, fucking it in long, deep motions. Seeing him abandon himself to this stranger stirred something in Claree and emboldened her to step toward Laura and stand next to her with her legs in a wide-open V.

Maybe Laura caught her scent. Maybe she couldn't resist unencumbered pussy. Claree willed the young woman's hand to her creaming lips and in seconds, that's exactly where it was. Laura diddled Claree as she sucked Nicholas. The couple watched each other's arousal catapult to a fever pitch—they'd never seen such wild-eyed horniness in each other that they hadn't themselves been responsible for.

Claree desperately searched for something to grasp as the throbbing pulse between her legs intensified and rendered her knees useless. Laura's shoulder was closest. The moment she clutched it was the moment the tremors claimed her body. Her shouts filled the room and even as she collapsed in stages beside Laura, her orgasm persisted, twitching and twisting its way to a close. Laura instinctively moved her hand from Claree's cunt to her asshole, spreading the juices from one hole to the other. After several applications of Claree's natural lubricant, Laura's finger rimmed her asshole, causing Claree to position herself on all fours. Her face was inches from the carpet, which smelled of patchouli and wet dog.

"Prepare to get fucked," Laura said.

Claree had her back to them but she knew that if Laura could speak, she was no longer eating Nicholas. When his thickness pushed at Claree's ready hole, she grinned and winced with a new wave of pleasure. While he inserted himself past her forgiving sphincter, the other woman got up and stood before Claree and Nicholas. As the couple fucked they watched Laura strap on the aforementioned dildo, which was the same shade of hellish red as her lipstick.

But she was watching them, too, and with every penetration, she stroked her dildo as if it were her very own cock. Her eyes glistened with ethereal delight. Her breathing grew shorter, like a man's would as his balls tightened with excitement.

"How can I help you?" she rasped. The submission in her voice came out in a plaintive purr.

"Fuck me in the ass, like you promised," Nicholas blurted out.

Claree couldn't remember later who moved whom into what position, but she found herself on her back, with Nicholas now entering her pussy. Her big tits bumped and jiggled as she absorbed his pounding.

Out of the corner of her eye, she saw Laura get behind Nicholas, whose body now obscured her movements. A minute or so passed, during which he pumped Claree's pussy, ramming himself so deeply inside her that he nearly tickled her spine.

But she knew when Laura's dildo poked its way into his hole. He paused, bit his lip, shut his eyes, and stifled a low groan. Once Laura was in and fucking he resumed his pumping, matching Laura's rhythm. He'd slam into Claree, Laura would slam into him. Damp skin met and slid against damp skin. Squishing, slippery noises sputtered throughout.

His abdomen tensed and his posture changed. Suddenly, his shoulders were larger. His chest rippled with muscles Claree had never noticed before. Laura's little grunts punctuated every new push up his ass. Claree knew he was close.

He roared when he came but the sound was nothing compared to the colossal pounding he directed into Claree's pussy. He trembled with demonic fervor, and seemed to want to pass that fervor along to his wife, as if the feeling was too much for one person to contain.

Claree came too, but the intensity of his orgasm blurred with her own and she couldn't distinguish which pulses emanated from him, and which from her.

Laura extracted herself from Nicholas slowly and got to her feet. She walked out of the room while her guests let earthly concerns gradually invade their thoughts. After several minutes, Laura returned, smiling, still wearing only her bustier.

"Take your time recovering. I think I'll just go to bed now, if you don't mind. Just go ahead and let yourselves out when you're ready."

Nicholas's eyes darkened. He looked like he wanted to say something but didn't know how. Laura recognized his hesitation and asked him if everything was all right.

"Oh, yes. Everything is fantastic," he replied. "But, I was, uh, wondering... Do we need to leave you any money?"

Claree hadn't considered the possibility that Laura did this for a living, or to supplement her living. She hoped Nicholas's question wouldn't offend her.

Laura smiled. "No, I don't do this for money."

Though her answer seemed to satisfy Nicholas, now Claree was curious. Laura hadn't come at all during the night, which made her voluntary participation all the more mysterious. What was in it for this strange woman with the tarantula for a roommate?

"So, why do you do it?" Claree ventured.

A beatific grin spread across the semi-goth girl's lipstick-smeared face. "There are very few lovers out in the world," she said quietly, zipping up her skirt. "They are so rare—like an endangered species. When I see people who are happy, I want to experience that happiness, know that kind of love. When I saw the two of you, I knew I could not only fulfill some of your fantasies but satisfy my own need for ecstasy, even for a few seconds." She walked toward the door to her bedroom, then turned to the couple one last time.

"Thank you for letting me inside." She closed the door behind her.

Claree looked at Nicholas, mute with understanding. Laura had gotten inside them in ways they'd never imagined.

ROGER'S FAULT

Eric Williams

It was Roger's fault that we were late.

"What a fucking day," he said, looking over at the piles of spreadsheets on my desk. "Let's go grab a beer."

I looked at my watch and shook my head.

"*One* beer," he insisted, and when I told him that I couldn't—when I said that you were at home, waiting—he asked, "What are you, man? Pussy-whipped?"

So, Christ, Elena—what was I going to do? One beer turned into two, turned into an hour-and-a-half of playing darts down near the pier at the Rose and Crown. By the time I realized how long we'd been playing, well, it was too fucking late to call and explain, anyway.

"We'll buy her something nice to make her feel better," Roger said, pushing me out the door to the parking lot. I shrugged uselessly. What could that possibly be? Flowers? Candy? No way to buy back nearly two hours of lost time.

"Trust me," Roger said. "I know the perfect gift."

Then we were back in his shiny black pickup, cruising along Santa Monica Boulevard, through the sumptuous curves of Beverly Hills, cresting into Hollywood. I had my hand on my cell phone, trying to think up some excuse that didn't sound too lame, but he said, "It won't help to call now. We'll just show up with our gift and smooth things over."

Roger acted as if he really knew what he was talking about, and it sounded good, the way he said it. But when he pulled into the parking lot of The Pleasure Garden, I honestly thought he'd lost his mind.

"Come on," I smiled, shaking my head. "I'm not going into a vibrator store with you." Roger didn't even answer. It was obvious that he'd leave me in the truck if I didn't follow, so I kicked open the door and trailed after him. "You're crazy," I said, but he ignored my words, making me hurry to catch up, tripping down the steps and into the wonderful world of sex toys.

What a sight we made. Two guys in expensive work suits, perusing the aisles of marabou-trimmed nighties, edible panties, inflatable dolls, vibrators, paddles, lubricant. Roger acted casual about the whole thing, as if he shopped in stores like that every day. And then there was me, late as hell already, not knowing what the fuck we were doing there.

"Trust me," Roger said again, this time hefting a huge ribbed purple dildo and poking around in a basket for a suitable leather harness, one that would fit your slim hips without looking foolish. He wanted to find a quality-made harness with a delicate buckle. Not too large.

"You've got to be kidding," I said.

"Elena will love it. You'll see."

"You're not buying my girlfriend a dildo."

"You're right," he agreed, and I thought I saw sanity again in my buddy's green eyes. "I'm not buying it. *You* are."

"There's no way."

"Chet," he said, "you can't go home empty-handed. She's going to be upset as a wildcat that you're this late as it is."

"So what?" I asked him, incredulous. "So I'm going to tell her to strap this thing on and fuck her aggression out on me?"

"Something like that."

And then suddenly, I understood. I'd been set up.

"She told you?" I asked, my voice cracking. I couldn't help but back away from him, standing against what I thought was a wall, but what turned out to be a display of artificial ladies, ready for a man to insert his cock in their mouths, asses, and pussies. Vinyl skin reached out to touch me, and I took a step forward, quickly, then whispered again, "She told you." This time, I wasn't asking.

"No problem with having a fantasy," Roger said, grinning now. He looked incredibly handsome with that knowing half-smile, his short dark hair, and a start of evening shadow on his strong jaw. "Especially when everyone gets off."

After that, he didn't say anything else. Simply grabbed the items he was looking for, snagged an extra-large bottle of lube from the display by the counter, and paid for his purchases. I have to admit, I had no idea what to do. First, there was the fact of my immediate erection, already making itself known against my leg. I felt as if I were back in high school, getting hard whenever the wind blew—or, more honestly, whenever the little cheerleaders danced onto the field for afternoon practice. Those tiny pleated skirts flipping up each time they cheered...what filthy mind created outfits like that?

And then there was the fact that my best buddy in the world knew that I wanted my girlfriend to ass-fuck me—and not only me, but to fuck him, as well. It had taken a lot of vodka before

I'd confessed that particular kinky fantasy. Never thought the words would make their way to his ears.

Yes, Elena, I should have known, way back when we were sharing secrets. I ought to have guessed that you'd do something like this. Always ready to push the barriers in life, which is why I love you. But, thinking back, I realize that's why your brown eyes gleamed so brightly when I whispered the dirty words that made up my most private daydream. In your head, you were already playing this out: Roger and me, on our king-sized bed, and you, the queen of the night, going back and forth between us. Dipping into us. Taking us.

But still, I didn't think it would ever happen.

"Come on, Chet," Roger said, throwing one arm over my shoulder and herding me back to his truck as if he were leading a drunken man to shelter. "Elena's waiting."

At our house, the scene was carefully set. You weren't surprised that we were late, because it was all planned out from the start. The two of you know me too fucking well. Roger was sure he'd be able to coerce me into a game (or six) of darts. And you knew I'd feel so guilty that I wouldn't even have the balls to call. Ten minutes later, back at our house, there we were, Roger leaning hard on the doorbell before I could get my key out, and you, opening the door in your sleek leather pants, tight white tank top, high-heeled boots. You looked so fierce, I could have come on the spot.

"Boys," you said as a greeting. Just that word. Your eyes told me that I should have known better. That I was too slow to figure things out. Before I could respond in my own defense, we were walking after you like bad little kids heading toward the principal's office. Roger was the ringleader, taking my hand and pulling me down the hall to the bedroom, showing you the present he'd bought and actually undressing you and helping you put it on.

Fuck, Elena, the way you looked stripped down with that harness. Your pale skin, long dark hair, midnight eyes alert and shining. I wanted—well, you know damn well what I wanted. But I'll spell it out anyway. I wanted to go on my knees and get your cock all nice and wet with my mouth, to suck on it until the silicone dripped with my saliva, and then to watch as you fucked my best friend. I wanted to help glide the synthetic prick between the cheeks of his well-muscled ass, to watch you pump him hard, stay sealed into him, then pump in and out again. I couldn't wait to stand against the wall, one hand on my own pulsing cock, jerking, pulling, coming in a shower on the floor. Not caring what kind of mess I made, because, shit, I was beyond caring about anything like that.

That's not what happened, of course. We were in the wrong, coming back late like that. Me, especially, since I had a will of my own. I could have insisted that we go back to the house on time. Could have at least called. No, you wouldn't reward me by taking him first, letting me get off easy as the observer. That wasn't your plan.

"Naughty boy," you said. "Roger, help me bend him over."

At your words, there was a tightening in the pit of my stomach, like a fist around my belly. A cold metal taste filled my mouth, and it was suddenly difficult for me to swallow. Roger's seemingly experienced hands unbuckled my belt, pulled off my shoes, slipped my pants off, and took down my black satin boxers. Leaving those around my knees, he bent me over the bed, his exploring fingers trailing along the crack of my ass and making me moan involuntarily. Calloused fingertips just brushing my hole. Never felt anything that dirty, that decadent.

He was the one to help you. The assistant. Pouring the lube in a slick river between my asscheeks, rubbing it in, his fingertips casually slipping inside of me. Probing and touching in such a personal manner that I could have cried. I wanted him to finger-fuck me, to use two, three, four fingers. I knew what it would be like to have his whole fucking fist inside of me. And, Elena, did I ever want that. Roger, behind me, getting the full motion of his arm into it. But then his strong hands spread me open as you guided the head of that mammoth, obscene purple cock into my asshole. And I wanted that even more.

Jesus-fucking-Christ, Elena. How did you know? I mean, I told you, of course, that night at the beach, draining the Absolut bottle between us as we stared up at the stars and out at the silver-lipped ocean. Your pussy so wet and slippery as you con-fessed your secret, five-star fantasy of fucking a guy. And me, harder than steel as I answered that it was what I wanted, as well.

But how did you know how to do it? How to talk like that? Sweet thing like you. Fucking me like a professional and talking like a sailor.

"Such a bad boy, needing to be ass-fucked," you told me, your voice a husky-sounding purr. "That's what you need—right, Chet? You need my cock deep in your hole."

That's what I needed, all right, and it was what you gave me. That dildo reaming my asshole, with Roger there, spreading my cheeks wide until it hurt. The right kind of hurt. Pain at being pulled, stretched open. Embarrassment flooding through me and making the precum drip freely from my cock. I could feel the sweat on me, droplets beading on my forehead as I gripped into the pillow and held on. Never been fucked before, never taken, and here my best friend was watching. Helping.

As fantasies go, you never know what will happen when they come true. I turned to look in the mirror on the closet doors as Roger moved behind you, saw that your bare ass was plenty available since you were wearing only that harness. He wasn't rough with you the way you were with me. He knew how to do it, how you like it. On his knees behind you, parting your luscious cheeks and tickling your velvety hole with his tongue. Playing peekaboo games back there, driving the tip of it into your asshole and licking you inside out. Making you moan and tilt your head back, your hair falling away from your face, your cheeks flushed.

Then he was the one to pour lube all over his cock, to rub it in and part your heart-shaped cheeks and take you. I had a glimpse of his pole before it disappeared into your ass, and the length of it made me suck in my breath. What it must have done to you. Impaling you, possessing you as he took you on a ride.

The three of us fucked in a rhythm together like some deranged beast. You in my asshole and him in yours. Joined and sticky, reduced to animals that simply couldn't get enough. I didn't want to watch, but I had to, as the three of us came, bucking hard in a pileup on the bed. Groaning, because it was so good. Better than good. It was sublime. Unreal.

But, in my defense, I have to say again that it was all Roger's fault.

Next Friday night, we'll be there on time, Elena. I promise.

YOU WANT IT?

Jolie du Pré

"Shakia, come in here and help me! Don't you hear me calling you?"

Shakia clenched her teeth and finished the sentence she'd been typing on her computer. *I gotta get out of here,* she thought.

But that wasn't possible, at least not anytime soon. She seemed unable to hold a job for more than two months, so she was always broke and there wasn't anybody else she could mooch off. When Alicia dumped her, after Shakia had been living with her for a year, she had nowhere else to go but back home. If she wanted to move out again, she'd have to buckle down and get her shit together.

She turned off her computer and headed for the kitchen. Her mother was in the middle of frosting a cake. The church ladies were coming over and everything had to be "just right."

"You spend too much time on that computer," her mother said. "Sit down and peel these potatoes."

What is this, boot camp? Shakia thought.

"I don't know why I agree to do this. I guess they all know what a good cook I am."

Shakia rolled her eyes. Her mother loved to brag about her cooking. Sure, it tasted good, but it left you five pounds heavier with every bite.

"Why don't you just tell them you don't want them over? They're all a bunch of cows anyway," Shakia said.

The look on her mother's face could have melted the frosting right off the cake. "Where did you get such an evil mouth? Certainly not from me. Why couldn't you be more like Donna? Your sister has such a nice life and a beautiful family, too."

"You mean why couldn't I be straight like Donna?"

"I don't want to talk about that."

"Okay, then let's not talk about it."

Her mother shook her head and walked away, leaving Shakia alone.

As she peeled the potatoes, Shakia planned her escape. After all, it was Friday night, and the Cactus, the hottest lesbian bar in town, was always jumpin' on a Friday night.

"I'm going out," Shakia shouted so her mother could hear. "So you don't have to worry about me."

"No you ain't!" her mother said, hurrying back into the kitchen. "Mrs. Dawson is bringing her niece Elise over. She's visiting from California. I've never met her, but Mrs. Dawson says she's a nice young lady. I need you to spend some time with her while the grown ladies talk."

"I'm grown, too, Momma! I'm twenty-four!"

"You know what I mean."

"But I'm going out tonight."

"You're not going anywhere. I'm tired of you runnin' the streets. You need to stay home and be a good girl like Elise."

Shakia sighed. She really missed her freedom.

The table was set beautifully as always. Shakia's mother paced back and forth, wondering what she had forgotten. She had on her flowered cocktail dress, the one that made her look ten times fatter then she already was. Shakia hated that dress, and that god-awful perfume she wore that permeated every room in the house.

I'm just gonna sneak out of here, Shakia thought.

The bell rang and Shakia's mother hurried over to the door.

"Praise the Lord! Y'all come on in!"

"Good evening! This is my niece, Elise," Mrs. Dawson said.

If Shakia could have photographed the look on her mother's face at that very moment, she would have. It was priceless. Elise was a large, tall, dark woman, with very short hair, wearing a men's black jacket and pants. If it weren't for the mounds on her chest, she could easily be mistaken for a man.

"You want me to take her into my bedroom, Momma?" Shakia asked, trying not to laugh. "We can play some games."

Her mother shot her a look, but then quickly put her party face back on as more guests arrived at the door.

When Shakia turned to talk to Elise, she was gone. Shakia walked to her bedroom and found Elise sitting on her bed.

"What are you doing in my room?" Shakia asked.

"Just chillin'. Been traveling all day, two different airports," Elise responded.

"Well, I wouldn't know about all that because I don't do airports. I'm afraid to fly."

"I'm not afraid. Security didn't find my strap-on, either. So it was cool."

"Your strap-on?"

"Yeah." Elise paused, looking Shakia's body up and down. "You never know when you might get some ass."

Shakia rolled her eyes and looked away.

"Hey...I'm just keepin' it real," Elise said.

"Well...don't look this way. I'm straight."

Elise smiled and let out a chuckle.

Shakia was a good liar when she wanted to be, but she couldn't fool anyone about one thing. Everybody knew she was a lesbian. The church ladies even had weekly prayer vigils about it.

"Well...even if I was gay," Shakia said, "you're not my type."

Once again Elise chuckled, but this time a little louder. And once again, Shakia had lied. Elise was her type, and to make matters worse, she even looked a little like her ex, Alicia. That had been some of the best sex she had ever had, right up until the moment she was dumped.

"You like it here?" Elise asked.

"Why?"

"People talk. They say you and your mother are always fussin' at each other."

"Well...I don't know that that's any of your business."

"Poor Shakia. It's Friday night and she can't come out to play."

"How do you know so much? And I can play. I'm skippin' this place tonight."

"What you gonna do, sneak out the window? Relax, we can play right here. I know a game."

"Oh yeah, what kind of game?"

Elise patted the bed with her palm. "Come over here and find out."

Shakia got quiet. "You've got some nerve. My momma's out there."

"You hear all that cackling? Your momma ain't thinking about you, girl."

"I'm gay, and I don't want no dick, fake or not."

"I thought you said you were straight?"

"I lied."

"I know. Tell me somethin', what color are your panties?"

"That ain't none of your damn business!"

"Are they red like your bra?"

"How do you know what color my bra is?" Shakia looked down at her chest. Some of the buttons on her blouse had popped open, revealing her bra and the cleavage of her large, full breasts.

"Yeah, I been peepin' at it, wondering what the rest of those tits look like, too."

"Well...I guess you ain't gonna find out." Shakia turned her back on Elise and walked over to the door. It was loud outside. More and more ladies were arriving. Her mother's voice was the most annoying of all, high-pitched and shrill like a baby bird.

But in her room there was silence. She felt Elise's eyes on her. Why do this? Shakia thought. Why deny the fact that the crotch of her panties was completely soaked?

She turned around. Elise stared her in the face, smiling and relaxed...waiting.

"You want it?" Elise asked.

Shakia's body grew hot.

"Then come over here and get it."

Shakia hesitated and looked at the door.

"If you're worried...lock it. Better close the curtains, too," Elise said.

Shakia walked over to the door and turned the lock. Then she went over to the window and closed the curtains. After she was done, she looked at Elise.

"Now get on the bed."

Shakia pulled off her shoes and did what she was told. She lay on her back, with her head on the pillow.

Elise stepped out of her shoes, pulled off her jacket and put it on a chair, and climbed on top of Shakia. She knelt over her,

careful not to crush her with her large body, and kissed her full
on the lips.

Such a soft mouth. *I could kiss these lips for hours,* Shakia
thought.

Then Elise opened Shakia's blouse and stared at her bra.
"Mmmm...they look good enough to kiss," Elise said. She lowered her lips to one breast and then the other. Then she looked
into Shakia's eyes. "Turn over."

"Okay," Shakia said meekly.

When Shakia was lying on her stomach, Elise pulled her skirt
and panties off and placed them at the end of the bed.

"I want to stare at that booty, so don't you move. Don't look
at me, either," Elise said.

"I won't," Shakia responded.

With her face in the pillow, she heard Elise pull off her pants
and throw them on the chair. She wanted to look, but Elise was
in control, and truthfully, that's just the way Shakia liked it.
Suddenly, she felt a slap on her bottom, causing every nerve in
her butt to tingle.

"Ohhh," Shakia moaned.

"You like that?" Elise asked.

"Yes," Shakia said.

She heard Elise fiddle with something. Then she felt Elise's
finger on her butthole, rubbing it with lubricant. Then the finger
went inside, slowly, in and out.

At first Shakia tightened, but she soon relaxed when she felt
Elise's hot breath on her ear.

"You got a nice ass, baby," Elise whispered.

She pulled her finger out and replaced it with something much
larger.

"Oh...God!" Shakia cried. She'd had dildos in her pussy, but
never in her ass.

Elise put her hands on Shakia's backside and pushed in and out of her slowly. Shakia opened up with every thrust. This was a new sensation and she welcomed it. Soon the dildo was completely inside of her.

"Fuck me!" Shakia whimpered.

She grabbed on to the headboard, her breasts smashed against the bed. Her pussy tightened and her climax built as Elise pushed into her fast and deep.

"Yeah! Take it, baby!" Elise cried.

"Ahhh...God!" Shakia shouted. Soon one spasm after another overtook her.

Then Elise slowly pulled the dildo out. Shakia lay on the bed exhausted. When she finally turned over, Elise had her pants on, just like before. They looked at each other and smiled, but the moment was broken by a knock on the door.

"Shakia... Elise?"

Shakia grabbed her panties and her skirt and hurried into them. "Just a minute, Momma!"

"What's going on in there?"

"One second!" Shakia opened the door. "Hi, Momma. Ummm...Elise was just helping me talk to God."

Her mother looked at Elise. "Oh...well isn't that nice. Thank you, Elise."

"No problem, Mrs. Campbell. It was a pleasure."

DON'T WAIT

Felix D'Angelo

I was already kissing my way down your body, my mouth watering for your cunt, when you said, "Don't."

It was only the second time we'd made love; since you'd so enthusiastically received my tongue that first time, this new reticence caught me a little off guard. I looked up at you quizzically and you said, "It's that time of the month. I'm sorry, I should have told you before."

You still had your panties on, and when I touched your pussy through the black cotton I felt the string hanging out. I smiled up at you.

"I'm still going to eat you out," I said.

"Gross," you told me. "Please don't."

"Not like that," I said. "I have something else in mind. I'll make you a deal. I'll start. You can stop me anytime you want."

"Something else?"

"Anytime you want, you can stop me."

"All right," you said softly, your voice small.

"Take off your panties."

You took them off, black cotton panties, so unlike the virginal white lace ones you'd worn the first time we were together. You were stretched out on the bed, and I was hanging halfway over the foot of it. I put my arms under your thighs and pulled you down on the bed so I could kneel on the floor as I lifted your legs up high. You were clean, but your pussy was, of course, dry. I gave your clit a gentle lick and heard you gasp and moan, let a trickle of spittle ease out so that when I curled my arm around your thigh and pressed my thumb to your clit, it slid smoothly. Then I pushed your legs up even higher, kissing down to the sweet curve of your ass.

"Jesus," you moaned as I let my tongue tease your asshole. "Oh, my god. What are you doing?"

"Eating you out," I said, and buried my face between your cheeks.

"Oh, god," you said. "That feels..."

"Good?" I asked, taking my tongue out just long enough to ask the question.

"I don't...I don't know, oh Jesus," you moaned, and I slid my tongue back into your cleft. You let me hold your legs open wide and up high, and I repositioned my arm so I could better stroke your clit as I put my tongue deep into your ass. I really should have asked first, I suppose—I didn't know if you were interested in anal play. But your moans told me everything I needed to know, and you lifted your ass off the bed as I pressed my lips between your cheeks. Your asshole tasted sharp, tangy, not unlike your pussy, which made me want more. I pushed my tongue into your tight hole and rubbed your clit more firmly.

"It's good," you said. "It's really, really good..."

I could tell from your surprise that it was your first time. I resolved to give you a rim job so good you would want one every day for the rest of your life. I drew the tip of my tongue in little circles around your hole. I slid the full length of my tongue into your crack and licked, firmly, just enough pressure to make your naked body shiver.

"Don't stop," you begged. "That feels good...."

I burrowed deeper, savoring the feel of your asshole on my tongue. I loved that I was making you submit to oral pleasure at a time when you had thought you couldn't have any. I rubbed your clit firmly, still learning the rhythms of your body but knowing that I was going to make you come whether you liked it or not.

You liked it. Your hips started to rock in time with my fingers on your clit, and when the ache started in my arm and my neck I barely noticed them. But I wanted it to go on forever, so I moved you into a place where I could continue. As I licked deeper, I pushed you onto your side and spread your cheeks with my hands, spreading them wide to allow me better access to your back door. Your hand traveled down to your clit and you started rubbing yourself, moaning loudly as I serviced your asshole.

"Keep doing it," you panted. "Just...like...that!"

I drove my tongue into you, my fingertips tingling as I felt the charge from your opened ass. Your asshole tightened as you rubbed your clit faster, and I knew it wouldn't be long before you came. You were playing with your breasts, pinching your nipples, something you'd told me you only did when you were about to come.

I licked faster. You were going to come, and I wanted it. I wanted you to come with my tongue in your asshole.

"Oh, god," you moaned. "Fuck, I'm going to—"

Then you did, pushing your ass back hard against my face, forcing your hole onto my tongue. The muscles contracted as you came, but nothing prepared me for how loud you moaned as you let yourself go. Your whole body twisted and you let go of your clit and clawed at the bed, ripping the sheets free as your asshole surged and seethed against my tongue.

When you'd finished coming, you gave one last shudder and reached back for me. Your hands were shaking.

I slid up your body, curving my arms around you and pulling you back against my body.

"Did you like it?" I asked you.

"Fuck, yes," you moaned. "Nobody ever…"

"But I will," I told you, whispering into your ear. "Again. And we don't need to wait till next month."

"Please don't," you said, and snuggled your ass back against me.

IMPRESSIONABLE

Chris Bridges

A person can only look for comfort in a mirror for so long before it becomes too depressing. Tonight Kathy lasted twenty-seven minutes, beating her previous time by twelve seconds.

There was no use for it. She had to go to bed sometime, and with any luck he'd be asleep by now. Taking a deep breath, she double-checked the buttons on her heavy nightgown, adjusted her curlers, and opened the bathroom door.

Her first thought was god, he must have rented a western this time.

Her husband Jerry was a good-looking guy, tall and broad and muscular. He was even good looking dressed as a ridiculous cabaret cowboy: skintight pleather pants, no shirt, leather vest, shit-kicker boots, topped off with a tall ten-gallon hat. He might have fit in perfectly in the cast of *Oklahoma!* or as a missing Village Person, but in their cozy little bedroom he looked absurd. Kathy looked around quickly for signs of rope and sighed with relief when no obvious lariats or branding irons presented themselves.

"Jerry, what the hell are you doing?"

He leaped off the bed to stand proud and tall, fists on his hips. "Howdy, ma'am! I run off those no-account varmints hustling your cattle and I'm here for mah ree-ward!" What his ree-ward was supposed to be was obvious, as was the wholly inadequate size of his pants.

Kathy walked past him to the dresser and pulled her earrings off. "Knock it off, cowboy. I need sleep." *I need a husband who doesn't think adult movies are guidelines, is what I need,* she told herself. She glanced over to the TV and saw the telltale boxes on top: *Hopalong Ass-idy*; *The Wild, Wild Chest*; and *The Slut With No Name*. Oh, god.

"But honey...," he caught himself and continued with his voice dropped down two octaves. "But ma'am, them cattle hustlers were tough to fight. I could surely use some first aid."

She turned to face him. "Uh huh. And what form would that first aid take?"

In answer, he dropped his pants to reveal a massive erection which, Kathy couldn't help noticing, was both throbbing and rock hard, as per accepted porn requirements. Had to give him credit, he did observe the details. He also clearly expected her to swoon, drop to her knees, and swallow something she had problems getting her hands around, and he seemed a bit put out she hadn't started yet.

Kathy walked over, took his hand (carefully avoiding the bouncing rod that curved toward her like a snake) and sat down with him on the bed. "Honey, we need to talk. Every night for the last three months you've been watching X-rated movies and then trying to act them out with me."

He beamed. "And aren't they great?"

"Yeah, swell. Look, the first few times were okay, all right? Even kinda fun: learned a few new things, had a few laughs. But it's getting old, and it needs to stop."

"Why? You'll scream with ecstasy as I fire load after load of hot man-juice across your face!"

She sighed. "No, Jerry, I won't. I'll scream when that acidic shit gets in my eye, if I can still manage to scream with my dislocated jaw."

"No problem, there's lots of things we can do!"

"Really?" She crossed her legs. "Like what?"

He sat up straight, warming to the subject. "You can go down on me, then I can go down on you, then I can fuck you and then flip you over and fuck you some more, and then get you on top of me, and then I believe I can either pull out and shoot creamy jism over your quivering belly or I can...um..."

"Yes?"

"Fire load after load of...hot...man-juice?" he said in a very small voice.

She patted his hand. "I think you're getting the idea. The stuff you're watching is just too limiting, honey, and I want to do so many more things with you."

"Like ree-ward me for fighting off the cattle hustlers!" he cried, bounding to his feet and waving his cock in her face.

She ducked and rolled across the bed. "It's cattle *rustlers,* you moron! Forget about the porn tape! Love me like you used to, or else."

"Or else what, little lady?"

"I didn't want to have to do this." Kathy scrambled off the bed and reached into a box hidden under the bed. "Or else this," she said, and produced a video.

Her husband laughed a mighty cowboy laugh. "A new one! Great! I'm open for new ideas! Maybe this one will let us skip that part about going down on you, huh?" He sat on the edge of the bed like a kid at the cineplex. "Come on, we'll do whatever this one does, right?"

She sighed, popped in the tape, and walked back to sit next to him. "You asked for this, you know."

The tape began. Jerry and his whanger leaned forward in unison on the creaking bed, so as not to miss anything.

She wasn't watching, but she could actually hear Jerry's jaw drop open when the movie title flashed by. "*Bend Over Boyfriend*?" he said. "What's that?"

"Ride 'em, cowboy," she said, smiling, and reached into the box again.

BUTTERFLIES AND MYTHS

Greg Wharton

Legend has it that whispering a wish to a butterfly, then releasing it to carry the wish to the heavens, will make the wish come true.

I kiss Trebor good night. A soft kiss on his scruffy cheek, then a whispered *I love you* into his ear. We are snuggled up close in our bed, him on his back, jaw slightly open, softly snoring, and me on my side, watching the profile of the man I love as he sleeps. Trebor's face is so sweet, almost prepubescent, with smooth soft skin, a striking contrast to how hairy my Bear man is. His pretty baby face defies his age—just last week celebrating his forty-fifth birthday—and gives the only hint of who he used to be.

It hasn't fully hit me yet, the emotions slow to catch up with the news that we will be separated for three months. He broke the news to me earlier tonight while we ate dinner.

"I got the *Geographic* grant," Trebor says while noisily chewing a mouthful of spinach salad.

"The *Geod*—" I hadn't heard him clearly.

"Yeah……NO! The *Geographic* grant! For my Itzpapáálotl expedition to Mexico for the winter!"

"No shit? That's great, babe," I say, hoping I sound cheerful even though I realize this means travel for him, and separation anxiety for me. I'm selfish. I can't help it. I didn't think he would actually go and I don't want his research to take him away from me.

"Don't be that way." His face is blushing red. It always turns blotches of red when he has to deal with my childish emotions. We've been together just over a year and he is just now beginning to truly know my mood swings. I'm what he calls a live wire, my emotions quick to jump from one extreme to another.

My face must have said it all. "What way am I—"

"You know what this means to me. It'll only be three months. Three months. What's that mean in the big picture? We talked about this already, baby. You knew I was planning to go and that I was hoping the grant could make it happen."

"I know," I say while pushing my plate away. Chewing on my lips and trying not to make eye contact, I pour us both more Protocolo, our favorite Spanish red wine. God, why did I have to act like such a child instead of the thirty-year-old adult I was supposed to be?

Trebor has degrees in zoology, entomology, and tropical agriculture from Oxford, London, and Reading Universities. He has studied *Lepidoptera*—butterflies and moths—most of his life and has collected throughout Europe, Africa, the Indian Ocean Islands, and most of North, Central, and South America. He's become one of the world's top experts on butterflies, specifically those in North America.

The *Geographic* grant covers the cost of an expedition to travel throughout Mexico, not to collect butterflies, but to collect and catalog the history of butterflies, including ancient Mexico's beliefs in the winged beasts and several goddesses, including the Aztec goddess Itzpapáálotl. This would take about four months total—three of those in Mexico—for all the traveling and cataloging, before his research finally being published. It was important to Trebor and I was being a brat, but I couldn't stop myself.

"Look—"

"No! You look!" I scream, throwing my plate at the sink. It lands with a thud, instead of the crash I had wanted. "Shit! I'm sorry, Treb, I—"

"I know, Travis. I know. I'm going to miss you something crazy. We'll get you tickets to come for a week in January. How 'bout over New Year's? Ring in the New Year in Meheeko? You can get away from the deep freeze for a little while. It'll do you good. I'm not going away forever, okay? I'm not leaving you. It's my job."

And that was it. Trebor's leaving for the winter.

Many ancient civilizations believed that butterflies were symbols of the human soul. The Greeks believed that a new human soul was born each time an adult butterfly emerged from its cocoon; Northern Europeans believed that dreams were the result of the soul-butterfly's wanderings through other worlds; and in Southern Germany, some believed that the dead were reborn as children who flew about as butterflies. The Irish believed that butterflies were the souls of the dead waiting to pass through purgatory, and the Shoshone that butterflies were originally pebbles, into which the Great Spirit blew the precious breath of life. The Blackfoot believed that dreams were brought

to us in sleep by butterflies; the Maya that butterflies were the
spirits of dead warriors in disguise descended to earth; the
Aztecs that the happy dead in the form of beautiful butterflies
would visit their relatives to assure that all was well.

And the Nagas of Assam believed the dead went through a
series of transformations in the underworld finally to be reborn
as a butterfly. When the butterfly died, that was the end of the
soul forever.

"How was your day, lovely man?" he asks me as soon as I walk
through the door.

I had been very sad and grumpy all day. And my job as Grant
Writing Assistant III at the University of Minnesota–Twin Cities
is stressful enough, even when I'm not in a sour mood. My day
had sucked.

"It sucked," I said giving him my best pouty-boy look.

"Sorry. You hungry? Or can I help you relax a little before
dinner?"

His bright eyes, naughty devil smile, and deep sexy voice—
as well as the thick cock he is packing down his left pants leg—
instantly make me feel better. Food is the furthest thing from my
mind. I need a good hard fuck.

Trebor leads me into the bedroom. He strips me of my
clothes. The touch of his fingers as they graze my bare skin
sends shivers up and down my body. I lie back on our bed with
my arms over my head and my legs spread wide, hoping that he
is as hungry for my asshole as it is for him.

He's taunting me, making me ache as each layer of clothing is
slowly and methodically stripped away: boots, socks, sweatshirt,
T-shirt, belt, then finally jeans. He leaves his briefs on, his cock
painfully tight and stretching the cotton like a tent, the bright
white of the briefs a nice contrast to his olive skin and dark fur.

"Show me your hole." His voice rumbles and a shiver shakes my body.

I do as he says, lifting my knees up and back so that my ass-hole is exposed and open.

"Ah, that's nice. So nice," he purrs as he rubs his finger lightly over my shaved pucker.

"Nnnnhhhhuuuhhhh—" I groan.

"You like?"

"Mmmmmmm......yes......fuck......"

And he forces his finger in. No lube. No warning.

"YAAAAAAAAANNNHHEEEEEEEEEEEEEEYYY!"

"Good boy," he says as he slides it back out. "Good boy."

Trebor rubs his hand up and down over his hard cock, making sure I know what he intends to do with it. And I'm ready. So ready.

"Baby—"

"Shhhhhh......not yet, pretty man. Not yet." He opens up the bedside table's top drawer and pulls out our bag of collected plastic, wood, and metal tit clamps. My asshole constricts a few times at the sight and I draw in my breath.

"Ahh......you like?" He dips his hand in and pulls out a silver- and black-toothed clamp, opens it and then lightly rubs the teeth over my nipple, causing it to harden instantly.

I reach back with both arms and grip at the railings just as he likes me to. He thinks of it as a nice cruel touch to make me hold myself in position without any actual constraints—though we do use them from time to time—and to make me conquer the urge to move out of position on my own.

"Very nice. Very nice indeed." The metal clip is dropped back into the bag and he pulls out two tiny pink plastic clips. Clips I know well. Clips that are misleading in their looks as to how much pain—and pleasure—they can inflict. He puts the bag on top of the table.

Trebor quickly snaps them down onto the very tip of each nipple and my entire body stiffens. Pain shoots from one end of my body to the other like a bright white light. I try to breathe deep and focus. I close my eyes. Breathe deep and focus. Breathe deep and focus. To let the intense sensation warm through me and to let the endorphins take over.

"Now, let me see that hole again."

I must have been too slow. He takes each clip in his hands and twists.

I'm on fire. I thrash my body and holler bloody murder, but continue to hold on to the bed frame. My cock is so hard. I open my eyes and look down and watch it bounce up and down as if possessed. I pull my knees slowly up toward my chest. *Baby, please......*

"Baby, please......"

God, put your finger in me now!

"......put your finger in me."

Trebor reaches back into the drawer, his eyes never leaving mine, the sneer I know as desire growing on his lips, and pulls out the lube.

"Such a beautiful hole. I will put my finger in you. And I want you to be a good boy and come for me. I think you can do that, huh?" He squeezes a generous glob of ForPlay into his palm and rubs it between his fingers. "Look at that cock. Look at it! What a porn-star cock you have. It's huge! I bet I can make you come without touching it. Wouldn't that be nice?"

It does look huge. I'm so hard, so ready, so wanting him in me. He *will* be able to make me come without touching my cock. He has before.

"Whose ass is this?" he asks, then climbs on the bed, kneeling in front of my ass and legs, immediately smearing my asshole with the handful of lube. "Is this mine?"

"Ya......yes—" I try to answer as his middle finger slides in, slowly, one knuckle at a time, until it is buried deep inside. "AAAAAAAAAH," is all I can manage.

Trebor knows me well. He knows every inch of my body, inside and out. He knows what to do to give us both the most pleasure. For me, that is having his talented fingers up my ass, massaging my prostate, and for me to look up into his eyes and realize that that is what gives him the most pleasure.

"Mmmm......how's that......good?" And he wiggles his finger back and forth slightly, making my cock both leap and leak furiously. I lift my knees back further to open up as wide as I can and bump one of the clips. I shake as a body orgasm erupts through me.

Since I've met Trebor, I've developed the most wonderful thing: I can have body orgasms—what many men, I suppose, spend years trying to develop with Tantric sex. With me, it just happens. Well, Trebor's fingers *make* it happen.

I look down between my legs at Trebor. His cock is standing straight up in his briefs, and I know that tonight he will fuck me. I need it. I need more. More contact. Rougher. Harder. Enough to hold me during his trip away from me.

His eyes stare piercingly at me as he methodically rubs my insides, first one, and finally two fingers, pressing and exploring my prostate. I can't take my eyes from his and he starts plunging his fore and middle fingers in and out in steady full strokes, each time hitting right on target and rolling over my spot. I am now moaning, long and unintelligibly, trying to lift my ass higher onto his hand, to feel more of him. More of him. More.

"Mmmmmmnnnnmmm......"

"That's it, baby. That's it. Come for me, Travis—"

"Mmmmmmnnnnmmm......"

"Come for me!" And he jabs hard, both fingers fully inside, and at the same time his other hand lifts and twists my right clipped nipple.

My mind explodes in harsh light, my eyes squeeze shut, and my ass clamps down hard around his fingers. My cock shoots, warm bullets of my come flying through the air and hitting my belly, chest, and his arm and hand.

"AAAAAHHHHHHHH!"

And again.

"AAAAAHHHHHHHH!"

And he pulls his fingers out of my asshole's tight ring then forces them roughly back in.

"AAAAAHHHHHHHH!"

And I look down at him as my final burst of come propels from my cock, hitting me on my chin. I start laughing, partly from the amazing sensation of release, and partly from my continuing ability to come like a teenager at thirty.

Trebor joins me with a robust giggle and roll of his eyes, then lets his fingers slowly slide out.

The orgasm is amazing, still flowing through me like electricity, still causing my cock and asshole to twitch in unison. But I know the evening is just beginning.

"Be right back," Trebor says, climbing off the bed, his heavy cock flopping in his briefs, heading to the bathroom.

His back is a blaze of color. He spent several thousand dollars, and a great deal of time and pain, having his back tattooed as a reward for landing his first research grant to collect and classify butterfly and moth species in Belize. It's magnificent: a full-color, clearly detailed rendering of a monarch butterfly, spreading from shoulder to shoulder and neck to waist.

The colors are vivid, still bright after many years, only slightly toned down from the hair he so proudly grows, downy soft, but thickly, over his shoulders and back. As he walks the movement of his shoulders and jiggle of his love handles and cute little ass make it appear to fly.

I watch him walk—and his monarch fly—down the hall to the bathroom.

"Gotta pee. Don't go anywhere."

No worry about that. Nothing could tear me from this spot.

Butterflies belong to a group of insects with a complete meta-morphosis. This means that there is a pupal stage and that the immature butterfly is morphologically different from an adult butterfly.

Metamorphosis can be described as a life cycle. It is a cycle, so it can be very hard to say where it begins, and ends.

My ass is buzzing and a little sore.

Trebor returns from the bathroom to find me still in the same position.

"How do you feel?" he asks.

"Mmmm......I'm humming."

"And that sweet ass of yours?" He grabs each of my ankles in his palms and pulls me closer to the edge of the bed, pulling the sheets with me and making me giggle like a child being tick-led. "Ready for more?"

I am.

Trebor pulls off his briefs and his thick cock springs free, bouncing up and smacking against his belly as it catches the elastic waistband, then settling down to its natural hard horizon-tal state. He strokes it firmly, a look of extreme lust in his eyes.

I reach over to the table and grab the bottle of lube, hand it to him, then scoot myself closer to the edge of the bed, my ass hanging over the side, my legs straight into the air.

"Fuck me, baby."

The bottle makes a rude farting noise as he squeezes out a generous portion of lube onto his cockhead. We both laugh, and he strokes his now slippery cock and aims it at my wide-open hole.

"How rude!" he announces. Firmly grasping my ankles in his warm strong palms, he lifts my legs fully up and apart, then expertly slides, inch by inch, into me.

"Rude!" I loudly agree, more on auto-drive at this point than anything else. It feels so good, so fucking good.

Trebor growls with each full grinding thrust. My asshole is completely dilated from his talented fingering earlier, so there is little resistance, just pure pleasure.

I grip his shoulders with both hands as he continues to plunge into me. I pull my neck and head up so I can watch his face as he fucks me.

I'm so lucky. God, I'm lucky. Trebor is so beautiful. Look at him!

"OH, FUCK YEAH, BABY! FUCK ME! FUCK ME!"

I wrap one hand firmly over the back of his strong neck for support, and let my other hand glide over his densely woven chest hair, at first softly touching each of his large pink nipples, the areolas so large, pink and feminine against his masculine dark fur, such beautiful contrast, then more firmly, pinching and pulling first one nipple, then the other, until they proudly poke out.

"FUCK ME! FUCK ME!"

And he accepts my offer, slamming harder, each time almost pulling his cock completely out, then quickly burying it fully with a slight lift, knowing it will hit my sweet spot each time.

"I LOVE—"

And harder, so that each thrust actually lifts me off the bed. I have to let go of his nipple.

"I LOVE—"

And harder. And faster. Trebor's face is now totally focused. He's drilling me with short, very fast, and rough jabs.

"I LOVE YOU!" I scream.

Without missing a beat, he pulls my feet together so he can grip them as one, and uses his free hand to yank on my cock. Forgetting that it had already come once tonight, it's hard and begging to do it again.

"I love you too, lover," Trebor sings to me.

I let myself relax back onto the bed, Trebor in complete control of my body and its actions. My left hand flails in the air, probably comic to see, almost as if I'm a rodeo rider on a wild bull, using my arm for balance, each brutal thrust into my body met with an equal reaction of the arm, over and over.

My right hand reaches underneath to Trebor's cock, to my stretched-out asshole, to where they are both now joined in earnest friction.

My orgasm is building, and all I can do is let out short and loud "AH AH AH!" noises as I feel his every inch pound into me.

I'm going to come. Oh, god!

"AH AH AH!" I shout.

And my shouts are starting to be matched by Trebor's.

"ANH ANH ANH!" He's ready to come as well.

I worm my fingers in under the cock's harness, careful of not getting pinched. I know him well: Trebor is very sensitive. It's better not to handle him too roughly. Instead, I just wiggle my fingers, then my complete hand up and underneath his cock so that he is pounding directly against my hand.

"ANH ANH ANH!"

"AH AH AH!"

"AAAAAARRRRRRRRRNNNNNN!" and my sweet Bear's engorged clit bangs and bangs, hard, fast, and fierce, against my hand, coming, he is coming, his cunt wet and warm, hard clit extended and oversensitive, banging against my hand, his body trying its best to continue both the plowing of my ass and the stroking of my cock, but he's shaking, every inch of him shaking and nearly convulsing.

"AH AH AH AAAAAARRR!" and I'm coming. The volume of my come is less since I have just come an hour earlier, but the sensation is stronger as my asshole grips, its ring clamping down tight and then releasing and clamping down and releasing upon Trebor's thick cock. He strokes my cock until, satisfied, I am done.

My ass squeezes him out, and Trebor falls on top of me. We shift our bodies back on the bed and curl up around each other, my back spooned in against him. We stay like that for a long time, Trebor still wearing his harness and cock, positioned up under my ass and balls, just holding each other, both sticky and wet, him kissing the back of my neck and shoulders, and me just letting the electricity flow out of me through my hands and feet, enjoying the sensations, and enjoying having Trebor hold me close.

Unlike most other insects in temperate climates, monarch butterflies cannot survive a long cold winter. Instead, they spend the winter in roosting spots. Monarchs west of the Rocky Mountains travel to small groves of trees along the California coast. Those east of the Rocky Mountains fly farther south to the forests high in the mountains of Mexico. The monarch's migration is driven by seasonal changes.

No other butterflies migrate like the monarch. They travel much farther than all other tropical butterflies, up to three thousand miles. They are the only butterflies to make such a long, two-way migration every year.

Trying not to cry, I lay my hand and head on his chest. I want him to go, of course, it is a chance of a lifetime, but I will miss him terribly. One more evening of being able to rub my hand through his thick chest hair, and smell his comforting musky body scent while I fall asleep, then he will be gone. I whisper my wish *Please come home soon* into his ear, then fall asleep, my head on his chest rising and falling with his breath, my hand cupped over his furry belly, confused and slightly afraid of how I will handle the separation, short as it may be, but knowing in my heart that he will, indeed, return.

SOMETIMES IT'S BETTER TO GIVE

Bryn Haniver

"I'm sick of being fucked."

Julie's husband, sitting across their living room in his recliner, lowered his paper and raised an eyebrow at her—she never used rough language.

"You heard me," she added.

He nodded. "I did indeed—but last night causes me some doubt."

He had a point. Last night she had been insatiable, demanding him in her mouth, her pussy, and her ass, only reluctantly letting him come. He'd fallen asleep with one of those exhausted smiles she loved.

But she'd lain awake for hours, restless and twitchy, trying to figure out what else she wanted. The twins were at summer camp, getting into trouble as only fourteen year olds could, but that was somebody else's trouble for two weeks. She and Gerry had a rare and cherished stretch of privacy and time for each other, and sex for the first three days had been energetic and deliciously loud.

Something was missing though, and she sensed Gerry felt it too. There was a restlessness. It wasn't that either of them was losing their looks—the streaks of gray in his beard and temples had made him even more handsome, and she kept herself in excellent form with swimming and yoga. She felt damn good, and Gerry had never stopped telling her how sexy she was.

So what was missing? Last night she had thought long and hard, finally succumbing to a fitful sleep. This morning, perhaps as a result of dreams bubbling through her subconscious, she knew.

"Okay, you're right. I'm not exactly sick of being fucked. I'm sick of—only being fucked."

"Right," Gerry said, slowly, waiting for more info. He taught history and English, didn't speak much, and had the patience of the ages.

"Sick of always being the fuckee, and never the fucker," she continued. "Of receiving, but never giving—so to speak."

"And you propose to ameliorate this issue by...?"

A small shiver went through her—he knew damn well exotic words turned her on. A decade ago she'd nearly creamed her jeans while taking the GRE.

"Get dressed," she told him. "We're going shopping for strap-ons."

They made a day of it, having a nice lunch in the next town over and then visiting a sex shop that was out of range of Gerry's high school students or her associates at the lab. It was a big shop, and the variety was a bit overwhelming.

As she took a harness and one of the exchangeable dildos from the rack, Gerry looked a little pale.

"I'm reluctantly deferring to your desires on this," he said, voice low so the other half dozen people browsing the wares couldn't hear. "But I have two conditions."

"I'm listening."

He looked at the wide display of colors and shapes on the wall, then turned to her. "The business end can't be too big—or even remotely realistic looking."

"Something like this?" she asked, grabbing a long, smooth, and purple dildo called Silk.

"Actually that's still too big."

"A compromise has been reached. Excellent." She made a couple of thrusting movements with her hips and smiled as he turned pink and looked around to see if anyone else had seen.

Julie reached up for a very large, very realistic-looking phallus called the Champ, holding it between her breasts and giving him a wistful look.

"Still, it would be nice to try something like this on for size."

Gerry shook his head. "Actually, you can't fully appreciate the joy of having an erection unless..." He gazed off into space.

"Yes? Unless what?"

"Unless you've got a beautiful young woman kneeling in front of you, back arched, sweet ass high in the air, her head turned back to look at you, her face transformed by lust and anticipation."

Julie thought about it—she had been that woman many times, but how would it feel to see it from his point of view? It sounded so sexy her pussy twitched.

"Fine," she said, holding up the Champ. "I'll use this to fuck the babysitter." Scooping up the harness and both dildos, she headed for the checkout.

Gerry showed remarkable restraint on the drive home. Amber, their old babysitter, was in her second or third year of college now but she was back in town for the summer, living with a couple of friends two streets over. They'd chatted just the other day in the young woman's yard—she'd been mowing the grass in short shorts and a bikini top.

Unlike Julie's tall, firm, and fit body, Amber's was petite and well-rounded, with large breasts and lush curves. She had a friendly, beautiful smile and had casually flirted with Gerry.

As soon as they were back from the walk her husband had bent her over the couch and fucked her silly. It was great when the kids were away.

They were twenty miles away from the sex shop before Gerry finally spoke.

"You want to fuck the babysitter."

"Don't you think she's cute?" Julie replied, teasing. "Besides, you're the one who said I couldn't appreciate it without…"

"I remember what I said. I just don't think you'll—"

"Go through with it," Julie finished for him. Would she? Gerry didn't know it but she'd spent some quality time talking with Amber in the coffee shop yesterday and the young woman had been frank about the fun she was having at college—and about her sexual adventurousness. She'd also mentioned several times how good her former employers both looked, and that she'd love to "catch them up on everything."

Julie got the big dildo out of the bag and began stroking it gently, smiling as Gerry's eyes remained riveted to the road ahead. "I'll invite her over for dinner tonight," she said. Gerry remained quiet.

Dinner went remarkably well. They had dressed carefully—Gerry wore teacher semiformal, looking quite dapper, while she had chosen a smart blazer top and loose-fitting trousers. Amber showed up in a snug, summery dress she saucily called a "baby tee." It was short-sleeved, cut high, and clung tightly to her full breasts. Julie thought it made her look scandalously young and sexy, though the purplish color was probably something only a college student could pull off, and reminded Julie of a ripe plum.

Conversation flowed, and Amber was more than warm toward her former employers—she was deliberately flirtatious. After dinner and some excellent wine, Julie figured it was time to take charge. Beneath her loose pants, the mid-sized Silk dildo was strapped on, pressing up against her abdomen and lending her some courage.

Amber was leaning up against the bar in the living room, looking at the latest pictures of the twins. Julie walked up behind her and put an arm on either side, trapping her.

"As you might have guessed," she said softly near the young woman's ear, "I had a reason for inviting you over tonight."

Amber didn't turn or tense up, she just said, "Oh?"

Julie leaned into her a bit, feeling the dildo as it pressed against her taut stomach and the top of Amber's ass.

"Oh!" the smaller woman said. "My, my." Now she turned, her hand reaching down to rub the dildo through Julie's trousers, pressing it against sensitive skin. Without getting a chance to think too much about it, Julie melted into her first serious kiss with another woman, soft lips and gentle tongue tasting of wine, larger breasts pressing against her own.

Gerry, who she knew had remained skeptical throughout dinner, let out a sigh at the sight. Julie wasn't sure how long her tongue danced with Amber's, but eventually she got hold of herself enough to break the kiss and step backward.

Amber was smiling up at her. "Well then, Mrs. Johanson. What are *your* plans for the evening?"

Julie stood up straight and said, "Fucking."

Amber raised an eyebrow at her. Julie allowed her lip to curl into a small smile. "There are two beautiful bodies with five inviting holes in this room, and I'd like to fuck them all."

Amber's jaw dropped slightly, and she looked over at Gerry. He shrugged. "It's her party tonight," he said.

A smile spread across Amber's face as she stepped forward and slowly dropped to her knees in front of Julie. Opening the front of the trousers, she took the smooth purple dildo out and slowly licked the tip. Looking down, Julie was mesmerized.

"It's very feminine," Amber said. Tilting her head slightly, she took the entire length of it to the back of her throat, then slowly pulled back, resting her head on Julie's hip and looking up her. The sight had been remarkably erotic—Julie could feel herself getting squishy.

"Have you ever done this before?" Amber asked her.

"No," Julie whispered. She could feel the young woman's warm breath on her thighs.

In response, Amber deep-throated the purple dildo again, this time maintaining eye contact. Julie watched as the phallus, her phallus, disappeared and then slowly reappeared. She'd wondered what it looked like to her husband when she gave him head and now she knew: it looked sexy.

"Gerry, get your mouth over here," she said.

He knelt beside Amber who graciously held the dildo for him, licking the side of it with her tongue. His tongue joined in and Julie was amused to see he seemed more interested in Amber's tongue than the dildo.

She grabbed either side of his head. "Ready for this, sweetie?"

Amber was grinning, but Gerry wasn't, though he opened his mouth for her as she pushed gently forward. Amber whispered for him to relax as more of the dildo disappeared.

When he looked up at her with resignation and trust in his eyes, Julie felt wetter than ever. She thrust slowly until the dildo disappeared completely into his mouth. What could be sexier than having your husband deep-throat you?

A few more slow in and outs and he began to get into it, his hands squeezing her buttocks as they tightened and relaxed with the thrusting. The feel of the straps and the dildo bumping against her were driving her crazy—it was time for some serious fucking.

She withdrew from Gerry's mouth and told him to pull down her pants. Stepping out of them, she walked over to the dresser, removing the Silk dildo and replacing it with the thick, realistic looking Champ. When she turned around, Amber said "Oh my." Julie squirted some lube onto it and began stroking it, still wearing the blazer. Amber stared at her.

Julie pointed to their thick area rug. "On your knees," she told the babysitter. Keeping wide eyes on the oversized phallus, the still-smiling Amber knelt down on the rug, placing her elbows and forearms on the ground. In the compromising position, her short skirt didn't quite cover her ass. Julie strutted over, went down to one knee and flipped up the girl's skirt.

Amber hadn't worn any underwear. Catching a whiff of a clean, musky scent, Julie was caught off guard by a rush of lust. When Amber arched her back and rolled her hips slightly, Julie stared. It was so submissive, so inviting—having been in that pose many times herself, she knew just what the young woman felt.

"Please fuck me," Amber whispered. Overwhelmed with desire, Julie knelt behind her, put her hands on that smooth white ass and pulled Amber's pussy wide open with her thumbs. Amber moaned, and then gasped as Julie used one hand to guide the head of the big dildo in. The young woman was sopping wet, and whimpered as her lips stretched slickly around the thick shaft. Grabbing Amber's hips, Julie pushed it all the way to the hilt, her own hips colliding with the girl's ass.

She pulled slowly back, fascinated by the intimate view of puckered asshole, sliding labia, and emerging penis. When she got near the end, she could feel Amber push back against her.

The young woman's hunger made Julie's clit burn and lent power to her hips. She thrust forward firmly, reveling in the cry of passion it elicited from both of them. Getting a better grip on Amber's hips, she began to ram in and out of her, fucking her faster and deeper with each thrust, the slap of skin and the grunts of lust egging her on. In what seemed like a very short time Amber's whole body convulsed and she shot forward, facedown onto the rug, twitching with orgasm.

"Wow," Julie said. Glancing over at Gerry, she smiled at his dazed look. "How'd that look?" she asked him.

He just shook his head. Amber was moving now and Julie turned to watch her sit up and pull her dress over her head. Completely naked, she lay back and spread her legs. Their eyes locked and the younger woman said, "More?"

She looked achingly beautiful and sweet and slippery. Julie edged forward on the thick rug, moving between legs that opened wider to accommodate her. Amber guided the big dildo in herself, groaning as it filled her, then reached up to unbutton Julie's blazer. Julie knelt, mesmerized by the sight of her big penis buried in Amber's labia. The view from this angle was entirely different from what she was used to. Julie gasped as Amber freed her breasts and then began pulling her down by the nipples.

Julie was overwhelmed by the intimacy of it, the feel of their naked breasts mashing together, Amber's soft lips on hers, the young woman's body squirming underneath her as the angle of the dildo changed. It was too intimate, but she couldn't escape the passionate kiss—when Amber's fingers reached around and found Julie's engorged labia she twitched, driving the dildo deeper.

Breaking the kiss with a gasp, her babysitter stared up into her eyes and whispered, "Fuck me hard, Mrs. Johanson." Clutching the young woman's shoulders, Julie did just that, timing her thrusts to the stroking she was receiving. Amber's legs clamped down on her and she could feel an orgasm brewing. As the pace increased Amber came, shuddering beneath her and trying to squirm away, but Julie was stronger and on top, holding her tight, ramming deeper into her at an angle that ground the big dildo against her own clit. In a frenzy of thrusting Julie threw her head back and yelled as her own orgasm shook through her.

"Wow," Amber whispered into her ear. Julie had collapsed onto her, both of them still panting. "Could you pull out now Mrs. Johanson? It's still awfully big."

Julie rolled off with a groan, the Champ coming out with an audible pop as she sprawled onto her back. She looked guiltily at Gerry, but he had a huge grin on his face.

"Bet you want to fuck the babysitter too," she said.

Amber giggled and Gerry rolled his eyes. "It's your show tonight," he replied.

Julie sat up. "All right then. Time to fuck some ass. Go get the lube, and get naked." She shrugged out of her open blazer as Gerry brought her the bottle of lubricant and began to strip.

Amber sat up abruptly. "You are NOT putting that," she pointed at Julie's immense dildo, "in my ass."

Julie grinned. "Don't worry, either of you. The remaining two holes will be fucked with the Silk and plenty of lube." Hands still shaking a bit, she removed the Champ from her harness as Gerry finished removing all his clothing. His erection looked as large as she'd ever seen it.

"Fetch the Silk," she told him imperiously. As he went to the dresser she held up the Champ—it glistened in the soft light, still slick with Amber's orgasm. She caught the young woman staring at her.

"Taste me," Amber said softly. Maintaining eye contact, Julie impulsively ran her tongue up and then down the big dildo, following its realistic shape, savoring the tangy flavor, similar to her own and yet different.

Amber stared longingly. "Can I fuck you?"

Julie shook her head. "Nobody fucks me tonight." She took the Silk from Gerry. "Now both of you, on your knees in front of me."

As they complied, she attached the smooth purple dildo. By the time it was mounted between her legs there were two inviting asses in front of her, one slim and firm, the other round and tanned. As she slathered lube onto her dildo both her husband and the babysitter were looking back over their shoulders, eyes apprehensive.

"Ladies first," Gerry murmured.

Julie chuckled. "Okay smart-ass—here it comes."

Serious now, he said, "Be gentle."

She was at first. With lube-covered fingers she rubbed him, pressing the sensitive area between his balls and his ass, slipping a finger into the tight hole. This was familiar territory. The dildo swaying between her legs wasn't though, and she eased it in very slowly, reading the tension, acceptance—and finally, lust—in her husband's body language.

After two long, slow thrusts and retractions, she grabbed his hips. "Are you ready?" she asked, her voice low and gravelly. Instead of speaking, he pushed back against her.

Julie fucked Gerry. Shallow at first, she pushed deeper with each thrust, accepting his need to keep it slow. When she began to bite the back of his neck he shuddered—and picking up the pace, she took him through one of the powerful internal prostate orgasms he occasionally had when she fingered him.

From the sound and feel of it, this one was considerably more intense than usual.

He collapsed onto his side, exposing an erection that got

bigger when she pulled out. "Christ," he whispered, his body shaking, "that was—different."

Amber was staring at them, one hand unconsciously fingering her swollen clit. "Give me a second to wash up," Julie told them, "and then we'll both fuck the babysitter."

Gerry groaned and Amber kept staring as Julie walked to the bathroom and quickly soaped and rinsed the dildo. Swaggering back into the room, naked and erect, she started giving instructions.

"Gerry—on your back. Amber—slip this condom on him and then hand me the Champ." When she had the big dildo in hand she rubbed its length along her sopping labia, bathing it in fresh juices, shuddering at the sensation. Amber just stared.

"Amber, I want you to straddle my poor, swollen husband and take him into your pussy. That's it—face to face." She watched as the young woman lowered herself onto Gerry, both of them moaning as she enveloped his raging erection. She stepped up beside them. "Lube me," she said, and Amber, now impaled on her husband, turned sideways to rub the Silk with more lubricant.

"Now lie down and lift your ass a bit." Gerry sighed as those big breasts pillowed against his bare chest. Julie knelt beside them. "Since this is about fucking and not kissing, would you mind wrapping your lips around this?" she said sweetly, holding the slick Champ up near Amber's lips.

Amber grinned before opening her mouth and taking the large head of it in, her tongue hungrily lapping at Julie's flavor.

Leaving it with her, Julie moved around to the back. It was an amazing view—she could see her husband's shaft disappearing into Amber's folds, and just above was her puckered brown hole. It quivered—and Amber gasped—as Julie fingered in some lube.

Kneeling carefully between their legs, Julie began to push the strap-on in. Amber tensed up and Gerry groaned—Julie retreated a bit, felt the young woman relax, and then began to push again. She was burning with desire and quickly developed respect for her husband's gentle restraint when he had anal sex with her. This time Amber stayed relaxed and the dildo slipped in past the tight ring of muscle—Julie used her hips to push it in slowly, moaning when they finally pressed against the other woman's ass. Beneath her, Amber was breathing in shallow gasps and Gerry seemed to be holding his breath.

Leaning forward, melding with them both, she whispered in her husband's ear. "Are you ready to give the babysitter the fucking of her life?"

His hips responded for him—she felt them drive up and in. Amber's cry was muffled by the big dildo in her mouth, but she squirmed provocatively between them and Julie began to thrust. She saw Gerry's eyes go wide—she knew he could feel her. Between them, their sweet young babysitter went wild, her hips thrashing and her mouth taking the Champ right to the back of her throat. Julie thrust and thrust, watching with awe as first Gerry, then Amber began to come. She rode them as they did, holding them together, grinding herself against the butt of the dildo and the ass of her babysitter until an immense orgasm washed up from the two squirming bodies and swept her into darkness.

Julie's vision came back to a tangle of limbs on the rug. She was on her back, her husband's head nestled between her breasts, his eyes closed. She could feel Amber's breath in her ear and her warm skin alongside. Tucking chin to chest, she saw the dildo jutting up between her legs—one of Amber's hands cupped the base of it, the other was draped across Gerry's shoulders.

"You know," Amber whispered, lips brushing Julie's ear, "I'm around for another three weeks. Maybe I could try fucking?"

Gerry's eyes opened, and Julie smiled.

TANYA'S TONGUE

Thomas S. Roche

"Take off your clothes and lie down," said Tanya, "I've got a surprise for you."

I looked warily at my girlfriend. She had that devilish smile that told me her surprise would be decidedly naughty, which was both a temptation and a cause for caution. I had enjoyed Tanya's naughty treats many times. The blow job in the back of her parents' car on a four-hour road trip as her mother hummed along with Burt Bacharach in the front seat. The unexpectedly ecclesiastical spanking when I was dressed up like a medieval monk for Renaissance Faire. The stripper she'd gotten me for my birthday.

But even though Tanya never went too far, when she had that mischievous look on her fine-boned face, I always wondered with some trepidation what was in store for me.

I had just come in from raking the yard, while Tanya sat inside surfing the Internet. She was supposed to be working, but who can work on a crisp fall afternoon when it's sixty-five degrees outside but there's that pregnant chill in the air that says it's soon going to be much colder? Those last moments of St. Whatever's Summer beckon to you for a final summer frolic before you batten down the hatches for winter, and in Minnesota you'd better heed that call. Tanya had taught me that.

She always left the windows open when she worked on the little laptop in our bedroom, and that pregnant chill had worked its way throughout the air of our little one-bedroom cottage.

Tanya put her arms around me and nuzzled her face against my neck. "Come on," she said. "I promise I won't bite."

Perhaps this would just be another garden-variety blow job, which was, without exception, never garden-variety when Tanya was involved. She lived to suck cock; she had an oral fixation that was, at times, scary. I had experienced the benefits of Tanya's oral fixation many times, and I knew that whatever she planned to do with her mouth it would definitely be interesting.

"Promise?" I asked her. "Promise you won't bite?"

"Well," she sighed. "Maybe just a little."

That certainly wasn't enough to dissuade me.

"All right," I said. "But I'm closing the windows."

"Of course you are," she cooed. "Because you're going to be naked for the rest of the afternoon."

"We need to go to the grocery store," I said.

"I got your groceries right here," growled Tanya, a little edge creeping into her voice. "Take off your clothes."

I'll admit, I'm easy to persuade when there's a hungry mouth breathing warm sex against my ear. I pressed my lips to Tanya's and felt her tongue seething against mine as she unbuckled my belt. I kicked off my sneakers and let my windbreaker slide off my shoulders, then pulled my T-shirt over my head. As my nipples stiffened I realized I hadn't closed the windows, but by then Tanya's mouth was molded to one nipple and her tongue was working magic. I moaned softly and forgot all about the chill in the air as she pushed me back onto the bed. She had my pants off in an instant and left them in a ball at the foot of the bed as she climbed on top of me and pressed her body to mine.

Wrapped in a pink cashmere sweater, Tanya felt even softer than she would have felt naked. Her arms trailed a cashmere caress down my sides as she seized my boxer shorts and deftly pulled them down my legs and over my ankles. I was hard already. Tanya's cashmere sweater landed on my face and I breathed her scent as she unfastened her bra and slid my hard cock between her full breasts. She licked the tip of my cock gently as she pressed her tits together and bobbed up and down.

"The windows are still open," I said weakly.

"Then shout for help," she told me, and her mouth descended fiercely on my cock, swallowing it all in one smooth gulp. I moaned as I clutched Tanya's sweater to my face, loving her smell on it. Her tongue flickered all over the underside of my shaft, and when she came up for air she lavished affection on my cockhead in a way that made me shiver, and not from the cold. Her hands traveled up my body and gently pinched my wind-hardened nipples as she worked my cock in and out between her lips.

"Roll over," she told me. "Time for your surprise."

If I'd thought it through, perhaps I would have known what was coming. But I didn't have time to think, and I've learned through experience that when Tanya takes charge like that it's better to give up control, because whatever she has in store will blow my mind.

"Yes, Ma'am," I sighed.

"That's Miss Bitch Queen of the Universe to you," she said. "Turn over!" She grasped one thigh and pushed hard, guiding me onto my side and then my belly. My cock pressed against the bedspread so hard it hurt. "Lift your hips," Tanya ordered. "I don't want you fucking this bedspread. No coming until I want you to."

I obediently lifted my hips, getting partway onto my knees and steadying myself with my hands against the bed. Tanya's hand curved around my balls and she squeezed gently at first, then harder. I could feel the rough fabric of her jeans against my feet as she crouched between my spread legs, but I could also feel the full, smooth softness of her tits against my buttocks. She started to kiss the small of my back as she kneaded my balls.

"What's the one thing we haven't done, baby?" she asked.

"Had sex in the Louvre?"

She spanked my ass hard, one single blow telling me not to be a smart-ass.

"I'll give you a hint," she said, her tongue trailing its way down the small of my back.

I realized what she was going to do just before she did it; while it was hardly the only thing we hadn't done, it certainly was a ripe candidate for doing. But I wasn't expecting it, and if she'd given me half a moment to think about it I probably would have said no. It's so dirty down there, so taboo. Tanya didn't even like me putting my fingers in hers, which is perhaps why I didn't expect her to launch into exploring mine with such ferocity. But what I really didn't expect was the way it would feel.

Her tongue slid wetly between my cheeks. I felt it wriggling against my asshole, and my eyes went wide as she burrowed deeper.

"Whoa, Tanya," was as articulate an exclamation as I could manage, and it went downhill from there. She licked my asshole with the tip of her tongue, then pressed the full length of it against my crack, swirling in tender circles as her hand squeezed my balls. All I could do was moan.

Her tongue came away from me and I felt her breath warm against my now slick hole. "You like that, baby?" she asked me. As she spoke her lips tickled the curve of my ass. "You like having your ass eaten? I'm going to tongue your hole until I make you come." Tanya loves talking dirty, and no one does it better than her. She molded her lips to my ass again and I felt her tongue delving deeper, firmly pushing my asshole open as her hand traveled from my balls to my shaft and gripped it firmly. She started stroking as she licked still deeper into my asshole, sending shudders through my naked body.

"Fuck," I moaned. "That's incredible."

"I know it is," she said. "I can tell by the way you're pushing your ass up into my face."

I hadn't even realized I was doing it, but my arms were now sprawled across the bed, my face and shoulders flat against the bedspread. My hips had pivoted and crept up high, my ass raised to receive her tongue.

"You're begging for it with your body," she cooed, her mouth never moving more than an inch from my asshole. "Now beg me for it with your mouth."

"What?"

She spanked my ass again, a playful slap.

"Beg for it, bitch," she said with affection.

I swallowed nervously; I had never experienced this before, and part of me was still deciding whether it was okay to want this. Tanya's good with that. She spanked my ass harder and growled: "I said beg for it, bitch!"

"Please," I whimpered.

"Not good enough," she said, spanking my ass again. Her tongue slipped out and tickled my asshole just a little. "Tell me you want your ass eaten, baby. Tell me what a whore you are for my tongue."

The truth is, I did want it. I wanted it more than anything; I couldn't bear to wait another moment without Tanya's tongue back in my asshole. I took a deep breath and did what she told me. "Please," I begged. "Please eat my ass."

"That's it, baby," she said. "More." Her mouth descended on my ass again and her tongue worked into my asshole firmly.

"Please eat my ass. I'm...I'm a whore for your tongue. Fuck me with your tongue." Her hand was wrapped tight around my hard cock and she was stroking it in a rhythm that matched her tongue's strokes perfectly. "Fuck me with your tongue," I repeated, and then I was lost in a long, low moan as she moved her hand up my shaft and rubbed her palm over my cockhead, lubricated by my pre-come. All the while her tongue kept working in my asshole, coaxing more pleas out of me. "Tongue-fuck me," I moaned, the words sounding strange coming from my mouth. "Fuck my ass with your tongue."

Her tongue worked fervently between my cheeks as she stroked my cock. I was so close to coming, it could happen any moment. I knew better than to reach down and touch it myself—Tanya isn't the sort of girl who plays well with others when she's got a hard cock in her hand. She never learned to share.

"You want to come?" she asked, her tongue only leaving my asshole for an instant. "You want to come with my tongue in your ass?"

"Yes," I said, not needing to be told that she wanted to hear me beg. "Please make me come. Please, fucking make me come with your tongue in my ass!"

Tanya's hand tightened around my cock and she pumped it faster and faster as she drove her tongue deep into me. She knew my body, knew the moment before I shot, and her tongue left my ass at the very instant the first spasms went through my body. She squirmed onto her back and by the time the come had pulsed up my cock, her mouth was there to receive it. Her lips closed tight around my cockhead and her finger replaced her tongue at my asshole. She gently stroked my hole, never quite entering it, rubbing in little circles around the tight pucker as I moaned in orgasm. The climax felt like none I'd ever had—the stimulation in my asshole created a whole new world of sensation, and it was more intense than I expected. Tanya's mouth suckled at my cockhead as I came. She hungrily swallowed and begged for more with her tongue swirling around my head, each stream fuller than the last until finally my orgasm ended, and the last of my come drizzled out of me.

Tanya licked my softening cock down to my balls and gave them a little good-bye kiss, then came up and pressed her body against mine. When I turned on my side and took her in my arms, kissing her deeply without concern for the taste of my ass and my come on her lips and tongue, I saw for the first time the laptop on the nightstand. She'd jostled it as she moved, and the screensaver had gone off.

The browser was still open, displaying a page with the heading "How to Give the Perfect Rim Job."

See, technology does make our lives better.

"Take off your clothes and lie down on your belly," I whispered to Tanya. "I've got a surprise for you."

SECOND BREAKFAST

Xavier Acton

I never should have let her walk in front of me. From the first step my eyes were fixed on her ass, and two miles out I just couldn't take it anymore.

We were lucky, I guess. It was almost—but not quite—off-season, just a few weeks after the weather had started to turn. This part of the Appalachian Trail was impassable all winter, and the tourists planned their trips for later in the spring. The trail was all but deserted, and I had no company on our hike except for Serena's ass, taunting me from behind her too-snug hiking shorts.

She always wears her pants kind of tight. I've never been able to get a straight answer from her as to whether it's a bona fide preference, comfort-wise, or if she just likes the way my eyes glom on to her derriere when I see it in skintight cotton, spandex or silk. If there was any chance Serena was going to leave that trail without a rim job, it was shattered the moment she selected those hiking shorts.

They were pale khaki, sort of a sandstone color. They were short—very short. I could see the legs of her spandex cycling shorts under the hem of each leg, as if she was trying to remind me her ass was there. With her narrow hips and slight but round behind, Serena looks like the athlete she is. Hiking the Appalachian Trail, ten rough miles a day, was just one more in a series of athletic challenges we'd enjoyed together.

But right then, two hours after sunup, I had another challenge in mind: how to get my tongue buried deep between Serena's cheeks. I spotted a little path leading off to one side, behind a copse of bushes.

"I think it's time for a break," I said.

"What are you talking about?" she answered, not even turning around. "We've only been going for an hour."

"It's time for a break," I repeated, and grabbed her shoulder. She stopped, turned, and after a quizzical look she followed my eyes to the little path, gleaning my intentions without even so much as a wink, nod, or hubba-hubba.

"Already?"

"Already," I said. "You shouldn't have worn those shorts."

I could see the little shiver go through her; Serena knows well what my tongue can do to her ass. She knows that my happiest place is kneeling behind her, my tongue exploring her cleft as she moans.

"Late breakfast," I said.

"Second breakfast," she corrected. "We already ate."

I smiled. "As I recall," I said, "you were the one who did the eating."

In such circumstances, Serena rarely blushes, but she did this time, no doubt remembering the way my cock had felt in her mouth as she blessed me with a sunrise blow job to quell my morning wood.

She put her arms around me and kissed me gently. "Now you're hungry?"

I reached around her and grabbed her ass, squeezing her cheeks firmly through the thin cotton shorts.

"Famished," I said. "Get out the blanket."

Serena turned away from me and danced onto the side trail with a pixyish sense about her movements. "I'm filthy," she said. "We've been on the trail for six days without a bath. You can't possibly want to—"

"It's all right," I said. "I've got a filthy mouth."

Reaching the tiny clearing behind the bushes, Serena shrugged off her backpack and began to unstrap the blanket. "Oh, look," she said, leaning over and picking up a condom wrapper. "Someone else likes the off-season, too."

"Litterbugs," I growled, plucking the wrapper from her hand and putting it in my pocket. "These motherfuckers should learn to take only pictures and leave only footprints."

"You do have a dirty mouth," she said, flicking her hands and laying the blanket on the hard dirt.

"Find out," I told her. "Take off your shorts."

Serena's eyes found mine and held them as she unbuckled her web belt and wriggled out of her shorts, pulling khakis and undershorts down in one smooth movement. Her pussy was untrimmed from the long trip, and I knew when I got close its smell would be strong—hardly a deterrent. Without removing her hiking boots, she pulled the shorts over her ankles and deposited them in a heap.

"Down," I said, grabbing her and hooking my leg behind hers. Serena yelped as I dropped her to her knees, catching her at the last minute so she didn't bruise anything. I pushed her forward. "Hands and knees," I told her, and she obeyed, positioning herself doggy-style on the blanket.

Lifting her ass high, she presented herself for me. I'd spent the last hour imagining her ass before me, and now I couldn't wait. I knelt behind her and pressed my mouth between her cheeks, smelling the sharp aroma of her pussy and ass, so filthy and unwashed from hiking.

"You're sure you're okay with this?" she moaned softly. "I mean, I'm so dirty...."

"Here's a news flash," I said, and slipped my tongue into her parted cleft. She gasped and then whimpered, pushing her ass more firmly against my face. She was indeed exceedingly dirty; I could taste her ass more strongly than ever. But I wouldn't have dreamed of letting six days on the trail dissuade me, and I began to draw my tongue in little circles around her asshole, my hand slipping between her legs to stroke her clit.

"Fuck," she moaned. "That feels good."

My tongue came away from her succulent asshole. "You're wet," I said as I eased two fingers into her. "You've been wanting this too."

"You know how I get when you put your cock in my mouth," she sighed. "I was hoping you'd want a second breakfast."

I forced my tongue into her asshole with growing fervor, and Serena stopped her smart-ass comments almost immediately. My thumb worked her clit while I fucked her pussy with my fingers, and I pushed her forward so I could more effectively fuck her ass with my tongue. The taste was more intense than I'd ever experienced, but something about it made my cock incredibly hard. I vividly remembered Serena's mouth pumping it hungrily first thing in the morning, and my mouth mimicked on her asshole the attention she'd lavished on my cock.

Serena leaned forward on her elbows, pushed up her sports bra and began to play with her teacup-sized tits. I could tell she was close already; I worked her clit and pussy faster as I drove my tongue deep into her. If she was worried about other hikers discovering us, she wasn't showing it. Her moans rose in pitch and soon she was pushing back onto me, fucking herself with my hand and tongue as she pinched her nipples.

Instinctively, I was grinding my hips and rubbing my cock against the front of my own shorts. For the first time I wished they were tighter, because I was getting close myself.

"I'm going to come," breathed Serena, and I fucked her faster, licking deeper into her ass in long slow thrusts between circular swirls around her entrance. I felt her pussy contracting around my fingers, and the tremors reached her asshole an instant later. She gasped as she came, then let out a long, low groan of release as her asshole clenched around my thrusting tongue. She slumped forward, her thighs spread wide, her exposed breasts flat against the blanket, her arms thrust out in helpless abandon. As she finished coming, I put my tongue as deep into her ass as it would go and savored the last contractions of her intense orgasm.

I licked my way up Serena's back and kissed the place where her shoulder met her throat. As I stretched myself out on top of her, she felt the hardness of my cock pressing through my pants against the delicious ass I'd just tasted.

She reached between us and wrapped her fingers around my cock, clutching it through the cotton of my shorts. They were already dampened by pre-come.

"It looks like you want a third breakfast," said Serena. "Or maybe an early lunch?"

"Why not both?" I said.

"We'll never make our ten miles if we keep stopping," she said.

"Then let's not stop," I told her, and she reached for my belt buckle.

SELLING POINT

Carl Kennedy

"And of course," said Michelle, "there's plenty of storage in the basement."

I looked at her, so prim and proper in her navy suit, the knee-length skirt shrouding her seamed nude-colored stockings, the jacket revealing just a hint of the lace at the top of her camisole. She was slim, but buxom, and she had buttoned the jacket just a little too tightly, showing the curves of her upper body. I wondered what those tits would look like out of that jacket, out of that camisole. I wondered what those hips would look like stripped of the conservative skirt. I wanted to know what those legs would look like spread around my hips as I fucked her.

"I would like to see the basement," I told her. "Would that be a problem?"

"Oh, no, of course not," she said, her pretty face lit up by a smile. "I'll take you right down there. It might be a little chilly," she said. "The heat's been off."

"I'm sure it'll warm right up," I said.

"I'm sure." Michelle was flirting with me, trying to secure the deal on this half-million-dollar house. "The basement would make an excellent gym," she said. "Once you get the heat on, of course."

"Of course," I said, following her toward the door to the basement stairs.

"Do you and your wife work out?" she asked, just a little too quickly, her voice shaking slightly as she asked the forbidden question hidden by a casual real estate agent's query.

"I'm unmarried," I said. "And I would be using the basement for other pursuits."

"Of course," she said, her face flushing as she realized that her veiled inquiry hadn't escaped the prospective buyer. She opened the basement door, flipped on the light, and led me down the long flight of wooden stairs.

"It's a thousand square feet down here," she said. "Quite useful."

The basement was empty except for the water heater and a built-in workbench. I looked at the far wall and saw the wooden panel with its single latch. Michelle stood nervously, well aware of the way my eyes were undressing her.

"What's behind the panel?" I asked.

"The panel?"

"That's a false wall," I said. "It's plywood. There must be something beyond."

She reddened, obviously embarrassed that she didn't know the answer to my question.

"I don't know, really," she said. "I never noticed it before."

"A good real estate agent should know everything about the house, shouldn't she?"

She covered her embarrassment with a girlish giggle. "I suppose so," she said. "Well," she added. "Not everything."

"Mind if I open it?"

"Be my guest," said Michelle.

I walked to the panel and flipped the latch. I slid the panel out of the way and revealed the darkness beyond.

"Gee," said Michelle. "I didn't even know that was there."

I reached inside the doorway and hit the button that turned on the light. Michelle walked up tentatively and peered in.

She stifled a gasp.

"My goodness," she said. "I......I guess they didn't empty it before they left. I'm......I'm really sorry, Mr. Simmons." She was getting flustered, shifting uncomfortably and shivering slightly in the chill of the basement. "I had no idea. I'm......we'll have these......these......these things removed right away."

I walked into the hidden room and twisted the dial of the tiny electric heater. It hummed to life, warm air blowing out. Michelle's medium-length chestnut-brown hair swayed in the hot breeze.

"I'm sorry," she repeated weakly.

"Amazing," I said, surveying the room. "Would you ever have imagined?"

"No," she said. "I......they seemed totally normal."

"Just imagine," I said. "You've got a business relationship with someone, and suddenly you discover they're......what they are."

"Yes, Mr. Simmons," said Michelle. "It's......this is really embarrassing."

"Would you have ever imagined your clients were so perverted?"

"Not at all," she said. "They seemed......they seem normal."

I walked deeper into the room, running my hand over the smoothly-sanded St. Andrew's cross, touching the manacles that hung from the top of the arms.

"Excellent construction," I said. "They spent a pretty penny having this built."

"I......I can't imagine why they didn't remove this in preparation for selling the house," said Michelle, groping for explanations. Her face was now very red.

I continued past the St. Andrew's cross and ran my hand over the leather-covered mattress. It was very hard. I touched the tie-downs of the four-poster bed built out of four-by-fours. I reached up and tugged at the pulley with its waist strap.

"They put a lot of time and trouble into this place," I said.

I walked to the smaller panel in the wall near the cross and slid it aside, revealing a recessed cabinet.

"Good Lord," I said. "They've left quite a collection."

"I......I'm really sorry, Mr. Simmons. I'll have it removed."

I ran my fingers over the array of floggers, canes, and paddles. I rattled the chains of the nipple clamps and caressed the straps of the harnesses. I tested the weight of the ball gags.

"They must have known it would be a selling point," I said.

Michelle stared at me nervously, then covered her embarrassment with a giggle.

"I guess so," she said.

"What do you suppose this is?" I asked, taking a harness off its peg and holding it up.

"It looks......it looks like......well, um......" She cleared her throat. "I don't know, Mr. Simmons. I'll have it removed."

I saw in her flashing blue eyes that she did, in fact, know exactly what it was.

"I'd like to try it out," I said.

Her eyes burned. She was short of breath. "Mr. Simmons?"

I gestured toward the St. Andrew's cross.

"It's a selling point, isn't it?"

"I......I suppose so," said Michelle. Then, quickly, she added: "If you......if you happened to be into that sort of thing." She nervously summoned another giggle, trying hard to imply that she wasn't, that she would never be, into that sort of awful, terrible thing.

"Yes," I said. "I'd like to try it out."

Michelle was so embarrassed now that she couldn't look me in the eye. She stared at the ground. "I......I can leave you...... um......"

I shook my head. "Please, Michelle. I'll need your help in trying it out."

Michelle wrestled with her professional scruples. "I......I have another showing nearby in an hour."

"Then I imagine you'll be late," I said. I gestured toward the cross again. "Please."

Her legs quivering, Michelle walked over to the St. Andrew's cross.

"What do I do?" she asked, her voice hoarse.

"You know what to do," I said sternly.

She leaned up against the slightly inclined cross, putting her wrists over her head and spreading them.

"Very good," I said. "Now take off the jacket."

Never meeting my eyes, Michelle shrugged off her conservative navy-blue blazer. I took it from her and hung it on a nearby peg.

Her full breasts stretched the thin material of her camisole. I could see she was, indeed, wearing a bra underneath.

I took first one wrist and then the other, placing them in the padded steel restraints and clamping them shut. I shot the bolts, feeling Michelle squirm against them.

I ran my hand up the back of her leg, squeezing her ass through that conservative skirt. Michelle was breathing very hard. I unbuttoned her skirt and drew the zipper down the back. It fell in a dark pool around her ankles.

She was wearing very conservative off-white panties underneath, and an off-white garter belt clasped to her seamed stockings.

I nudged the skirt with my toe. Michelle stepped out of it and I kicked the garment across the room.

I went to the cabinet and selected a paddle. Michelle's eyes were wide as she watched me return to her.

I bent down and took hold of her ankles. Michelle did not resist as I fitted her ankles into the padded metal of the cross's built-in manacles. I could hear her breathing, mingling with the hum of the heater.

"Are you warm enough?"

"Yes," she said softly. "Quite."

When I had her restrained, I ran the paddle up the back of her bare thighs and slipped it under the waistband of her panties. She squirmed.

"This certainly is a selling point," I said, and spanked her.

She gasped and yelped, squirming against the cross and pulling at the manacles. Her breath came quicker as I spanked her again. When I hit her a third time, she moaned softly.

"Excellent workmanship," I said. "Obviously the last residents had good taste."

"Obviously," said Michelle.

I returned to the panel and took down a flogger. A moan escaped the realtor's lips as she saw it.

"A good flogging can't be performed with your shirt on," I said. "I trust that's not too expensive a camisole?"

"N......not really," she said.

I took a shimmering knife off its pegs and came up behind Michelle, running the tip of the knife over the back of her neck. She shivered. I nudged the knife under her top and swiftly cut it down the back. I slit the sleeves and pulled the shredded garment off of her, running the knife edge over her back.

"Oh, god," she moaned.

"Have you ever fucked a prospective buyer before?" I asked her.

"Before?" she breathed.

"Yes," I said. "Surely you realize you're the one in chains."
I slit her bra at the back and the shoulders, and the off-white
lace fell away, revealing her full, perfect tits.

She moaned again, pulling against the restraints. I put my arm
around her and felt her breasts, caressing them and pinching the
nipples. I grabbed her hair, which was pinned in a conservative
bun, and pulled out the hairpin. My fingers tangled in her hair
and I pulled her head back so that, towering over her, I could
press my lips to hers, violently, demandingly. My tongue forced its
way into her mouth and she quivered against me as I explored her.

"Say 'please,' " I told her when our lips parted.

Her lips moved, but no sound came out. It was all right: I could
read lips.

I drew the knife slowly down her back and slit the sides of
her panties. When I pulled the ruined underwear out from between
her thighs, I pushed the crotch into her face. It was soaked. I tossed
the shredded panties away and brought my hand down between
her and the cross. I touched her cunt and found it shaved, warm,
and dripping. There was a ring through her clitoral hood and
three rings through each of her swollen lips.

"Playing hard to get," I whispered. "While the whole time
you were hoping I'd bring you in here."

"I'm sorry," she whimpered.

"Sorry won't cut it," I told her. I stepped back, returned the
knife to its pegs and took my place behind her.

"Please," she moaned.

The flogger swished through the air and Michelle's body
twitched. Her moans rose in pitch as I flogged first her back,
then her ass. Soon she was pressing back into the slashes of
the leather tails, gasping with each strike. I reached between her
legs and found her wetter than ever. She moaned as I eased two

fingers inside her pussy. I pulled them out and forced my wet fingers into her mouth. She licked them obediently.

"Impertinent little realtor," I said. "Begging for a flogging. We've got to shut you up on both ends."

Michelle strained against the bonds, twisting her head so she could watch me as I selected the leather harness I'd shown her earlier, and fitted into it the very largest dildo from the recessed case. I toyed with the idea of inserting a second dildo for her, but decided she would have to provide for me somehow. I slicked up the dildo with lube from a handy bottle and walked over to her.

"Please," she begged. "That one's too big."

"I doubt it," I said, easing the dildo between her lips and forcing it in with a single thrust. Her eyes went wide and she moaned uncontrollably as I wrestled the shaft into place.

I buckled the harness around her. Its designer had thoughtfully left the back quite unobstructed, leaving Michelle's pretty ass revealed—including her little rosebud. I returned for the ball gag.

"Now you can moan all you like," I said as I forced the gag into her open mouth and buckled it behind her head.

The harness and gag did nothing to quiet Michelle's pleas. If anything, freed from the need for self-control, she screamed and moaned louder. The flogger swished through the air and Michelle's back and ass were striped with angry red by the time I took down the cane.

Her eyes were very wide, now, the fear evident as I teased her cheeks open and nudged the tip of the cane into her asshole. She squirmed against it and tried to beg for mercy, but the ball gag prevented her. I gave her a single cane stroke and the sobs broke through as her lovely body, nude except for garter belt and stockings, was subjected to the most painful implement in this dungeon. Liberated from her mind's control, her body twisted in the manacles and thrust itself hard against the St. Andrew's cross.

By the time I felt my cock surging, aching, begging for that tight asshole of hers, I had left twelve parallel stripes down each side of her, from the first swell of her ass to the smooth bottoms of her upper thighs. Tears stained her face and her body was moist with sweat. I unbuckled her gag, grasped her hair, and pulled her head back, kissing her violently again, my cock grinding against her pained ass and making her whimper in pain as my suit pants abraded her freshly-administered welts.

"Are you ready to be fucked?" I growled, as I pulled my lips from hers with some difficulty. Her lips continued to work hungrily, her tongue thrust out as, famished, she sought more of my kisses.

"Yes," she whispered. "Please."

"I'm going to fuck you in the ass," I told her. "Put it up in the air for me."

I shot the bolts of the manacles, feeling Michelle slump into my grasp. I steadied her and she walked, her legs quivering, around the side of the cross to the leather-covered bed. Looking over her shoulder at me, she climbed onto the bed on her hands and knees and lifted her ass high.

"Higher," I told her. "Put it up high and beg me to fuck you."

Obediently, Michelle clawed at the leather with her hands and lowered her upper body to the mattress. Her ass rose high into the air. I could see the glittering silver of her pussy rings showing around the strap of the dildo harness. Her cheeks spread as she leaned forward. A woman's asshole had never looked so good.

"Please," she begged. "Please fuck me."

"I can't fuck you," I said. "Your cunt is stuffed full."

"Fuck me in the ass," she said. "Please."

"Spread them."

Leaning on her shoulders, her face pressed to the leather mattress, Michelle reached behind her and parted her full ass-cheeks with her fingertips, exposing her tiny asshole. Seizing the bottle of lube, I lunged for the bed, opening my pants.

"Please," she repeated in a whisper as the cold stream of lubricant drizzled into her crack. She moaned as I opened her up with my fingers, and by the time I slid my shaft into her I knew Michelle had a well-trained ass. She pushed up against me, her fingers still parting her cheeks wide for me, giving me unchecked access to her tight asshole. I reached under her and pushed the dildo more firmly into her cunt, using my hand to grind the harness against her clit. Michelle's mouth opened wide and she appeared about to scream as she pulsed toward her orgasm, but no sound came out at first. Then a strangled moan of pleasure exploded from her as I felt her asshole clenching rhythmically in orgasmic spasms around my cock.

I pumped into her faster, knowing I would come any second. Just as she finished her climax, I exploded into her, filling the realtor's asshole with my come.

When I pulled my cock out of her, Michelle slumped forward, exhausted, a sheen of sweat covering her body in the now-warm dungeon.

I lay on top of her and grasped her hair, turning her head to the side so I could kiss her.

"How did you know this room was here?" she asked when I relinquished my hold on her moist lips.

"I know the seller," I told her. "Charles mentioned you were a personal......friend."

"Then I suppose you don't want to buy the place," she said sadly.

"On the contrary," I told her. "I think you've earned your commission."

"Would you like to see the upstairs?" she asked me breath-lessly.

"I think you've shown me all the selling points I care about," I told her. "Let's draw up the paperwork. But leave the harness on as you do."

"Yes, Sir," she said, and I pressed my lips to hers again, vio-lently taking her mouth as I heard those words I loved to hear. Especially from a realtor.

CINDY'S DOWRY

Jean Roberta

"What did Harv have to say this time?" Shel asked her girl-friend Cindy. Shel believed that anyone who dates femmes must be able to tolerate a lot, and Cindy's long-term friendship with a flaming queen was one of the things she tolerated. However, Shel refused to join Cindy on her rescue missions when Harv phoned her with his latest tale of woe.

"He gave me some of his sex books. I didn't want to take them, but he insisted. I think he thinks he's dying." Cindy was obviously worried. She admired Harv's taste in makeup, hairstyles, and home decorating, although they disagreed furiously about whether the miniskirts and paisley prints of the 1960s were really making a comeback.

Shel was moved by Cindy's concern, and exasperated with Harv. "He usually thinks he's dying, especially when he hasn't been laid for a while," Shel pointed out.

Shel knew that Harv refused to be tested for HIV because he claimed that he didn't want to know, but every time he came down with a cold or a hangover, he wondered if this was the beginning of the end. He had already asked Cindy to be the executor of his will. He wanted to make sure that a trustworthy person would intervene if his parents tried to bury him in a suit instead of the satin gown he had already picked out.

Shel watched Cindy carry a box of Harv's stuff to the spare room, where it would join the rest of the gifts from Harv: jewelry, fabric flowers, hair accessories, posters, theater programs, books, magazines, and framed prints. Shel referred to the growing pile of Harv's souvenirs as Cindy's dowry, since she already had some of it when she and Shel moved in together six months before.

"Cindy" was Harv's nickname for the woman whose parents knew her as Maureen. He had once called her "Cinderella," and she had adopted the name. He considered himself her fairy godmother.

Shel liked to watch Cindy walking away since she had the shapeliest ass Shel could ever remember seeing. Cindy was small but curvy, with chestnut hair in short, sassy spikes, olive-toned skin that tanned easily, and a body that looked good in clingy tops and low-slung pants. Cindy worried about the possibility of becoming a fat, sloppy middle-aged woman. Like her dear friend Harv, she tended to see small signs (a little bloating during her period) as possible omens of worse to come. Shel's heartfelt assurances that Aphrodite herself, or any goddess at all, could not look sexier than Cindy didn't always comfort her enough. Sex usually worked better.

Shel glanced at herself in the hall mirror as she followed her high-maintenance babe into the spare room.

Shel was tall and slim, with a graceful walk. She was a long-distance runner and bike rider, and she valued her own stamina much more than the cheap compliments of admirers who tended to swoon over her svelte Nordic blondeness. She would have consented to being turned into a troll to pay for the privilege of spending a day in the sun without risking a sunburn.

"You don't have to keep it all, you know," Shel reminded Cindy. "Harv gives you the things he doesn't want so he won't have to get rid of them himself."

"You don't know him," Cindy retorted. "Look at this." She held out a porn magazine for gay men, opened to a cartoon showing a wincing, muscular guy, wearing only a T-shirt, bent over the hood of a police car with an even more muscular, leering cop pressed against him. The cop wore a jacket with a large badge on it. A motorcycle was parked in the background. The caption read: *Sorry, Officer, I didn't know I was going ninety.*

Shel snickered. "Oh man," she sighed. "Men. And Harv thought you would like to see this why?"

Cindy was fidgeting in a way that Shel recognized, while her cheeks were a healthy shade of rose. "Don't you think it's kind of—you know, Shel—kind of hot?"

Shel wrapped an arm around Cindy's waist. "For ass-fucking fags, yes, honey. That's what they like. It's crude, it shows an authority figure abusing his power over a reckless prick who probably deserves it. As long as they keep it to themselves, it's fine with me."

Cindy looked embarrassed and disappointed. Shel realized that there were pockets and corners in Cindy's psyche that she had never even suspected before. "Baby," she said gently, "you wouldn't really want to be a gay guy, would you? The bad boy who gets caught, or the pig who dishes it out?"

Cindy couldn't help laughing. "No, I don't want to be a guy, honey. I have some other stuff to show you, though. Some of Harv's books have women in them." Cindy rummaged through the pile.

She handed Shel a glossy magazine featuring an unbelievably glamorous woman wearing an unzipped leather jacket and nothing else. She was straddling a motorcycle under the title *Dykes on Bikes* in gothic script. Shel laughed aloud.

"You have to see the photo spread," said Cindy. She couldn't look Shel in the eyes.

"Bring it on." Shel pulled Cindy close to her.

The magazine fell open to a two-page scene of naked women with various skin colors lounging, sitting with breasts thrust out, cuddled together and leaning against trees in a green landscape that looked like the Garden of Eden. Cindy turned the page with shaky fingers.

Shel was amused to see the warmly lit photo of a blonde's round pink bottom in the center of a page that showed her sprawled over the knees of an older-looking lanky brunette with high, pointed breasts, an upraised hand, and a wicked grin.

"Mm," remarked Shel. "Someone's getting a spanking." She slid a hand down to Cindy's warm butt. "Are you sure you got this from Harv?"

"Oh yes. He says he loves to look at lesbian sex. He wants to know what we do."

Shel snickered. "Is this what we do, honey? Have orgies and spank each other in the great outdoors?"

"We could do some of it." Cindy was breathing faster than usual. "There's more."

A slim paperback book named *Enema Magic* gave point-by-point instructions for giving an enema, complete with diagrams and photos of several men and women shown from the back, with tubes disappearing into the cracks between their yielding cheeks. In some photos, other people held the bags.

Shel found the images and the text too medical for her taste, but Cindy's obvious interest in the topic was contagious. Shel was beginning to think of Cindy's delectable bottom as an unexplored country.

Looking for something else, Shel noticed a large, full-color coffee-table book (for book-collectors with no discretion, she thought) titled *The Back Door: A History of Anal Play*. The pictures ranged from images of vaguely smiling men pumping other smiling men on red-figured Greek vases made in the fifth century before Christ to devils with leering faces on their bottoms in medieval paintings of Hell to Victorian maids raising their petticoats for the inspection of the butler or the master of the house to a naked woman with a contemporary haircut and a strap-on dildo approaching a naked man bent over a padded bench. Between the pictures were pages and pages of print, organized in chapters named "The Ancient World," "Christianity and Sexual Sin," "Fundamental Rites," "Mollies and Posing Sodomites," "The Virtuous Alternative," "Investigation and Punishment," "Sexual Liberation," and "Gender-bending."

Shel was amazed that so much could be said about a form of sex that she had never thought much about. She realized that she had always associated it with childish gay men who still told potty jokes, and who liked to make messes. Harv's library of reading matter showed Shel how much she hadn't known.

As she and Cindy turned pages together, Shel's anus tingled and fluttered. She couldn't make it behave, or pull her awareness away from that area.

"Harv is really interested in this stuff, isn't he?" Cindy didn't answer in words. Shel pressed on. "He gave you a whole library on ass-play, Cindy. I'd like to know why. Did he want to do something to you? Did you let him?"

Shel's voice sounded harsher than she intended, and Cindy pulled away stiffly. "You don't understand," she answered.

"I'd like to understand, honey," Shel explained, gently pulling Cindy back to her side. "I'm not blaming you for anything, but I'd like to know what's going on. If you explain it to me, I'll listen. I promise. Let's go sit down." She led the way into the front room.

"Harv and I don't have sex, Shel," Cindy explained as though this should have been obvious. "He likes men. We're really good friends, and we like to talk. We tell each other our dreams and fantasies." Cindy paused, but Shel knew there was more, so she waited patiently. "I asked Harv what he knew about—uh, what you call ass-fucking. I thought he would know. So he showed me his stuff. He's even got some instructional videos and porn films that you haven't seen. He gave me the stuff he wanted me to have, but he still has more."

"So he gives you books to read for homework, instead of showing you what he does?"

"Well, yeah. You could put it that way. I asked him about it, Shel. I love what you do to me, what we do together, but I'd like to try some new things. I can't stop thinking about—you know."

"Something up your rear," Shel said in a voice full of wonder. "Enemas to clean you out in there. Spankings on your bare bum." Shel felt as if someone she thought she knew had suddenly given her a much bigger present than she was expecting. She wanted to pull Cindy's pants off immediately, and pull her over her lap.

"You have a beautiful ass, honey. Did you know that? I bet you didn't, since you can't see it, but I've been watching it ever since we met. And it's been so neglected." Shel realized the truth of this as she said it, and she felt ashamed of her formerly biased approach. As an animal lover and veterinarian's assistant in her youth, Shel had overcome her squeamishness about body waste and body orifices, even in bodies that were very different from hers. She realized that no part of Cindy's healthy female body could disgust her.

In a rush of understanding, Shel saw how it was. She could sense Cindy's fear that offering her virgin ass, inside and outside, to her respectable lover might drive her away. This was why Cindy had talked to her best friend about it first, to gain knowledge and courage. Harv, as a shamelessly queer man, seemed less likely to faint, cry, vomit, or erupt in rage in response to Cindy's persistent desires. Shel could see that if worst came to worst, Cindy was more willing to lose Harv as a friend than to lose Shel's love.

Shel felt overwhelmed with sympathy, but she knew that wasn't what Cindy needed most. "Stand up, honey," Shel ordered. She couldn't keep the grin off her face, knowing how much fun lay ahead of her. "Now take all your clothes off. Do it slowly. I want to enjoy the show."

Cindy couldn't stop grinning either, even though her face was red. Like an exotic dancer, she teased her audience by stroking her own breasts briefly before unbuttoning her striped blouse from the top down, button by button. When her blouse hung open, exposing her turquoise cotton bra (Cindy didn't like pastel underwear, claiming she wasn't a "beige person"), she pulled off her blouse and reached behind her back to unhook her own bra. She did this with impressive grace, and set her breasts free. Her rosy nipples were as hard as cherry pits.

"Nice," Shel responded.

Cindy unbuckled her belt, and paused. She looked as if she might hand it to Shel to use on her tender skin, but instead she coiled it neatly and dropped it on the floor. Cindy wiggled a little, then pushed her pants and turquoise panties off. Cindy showed Shel that she could balance on one foot while taking off her socks.

"Why do I ever let you wear clothes in the house, babe?" Shel asked rhetorically. "I think we'll have to have a new rule about that. Now I want you to bring me something. I'm sure you've played with some little anal toy. What do you push up your own sweet butt when you have the urge?"

Cindy's face showed that she had not expected Shel to understand so much. "Uh," she started. She wrung her hands together in a way that Shel found charming. "I have a plumber's candle. I dip it in cooking oil, and that, um, helps it get in."

Shel stood up and wrapped Cindy in her arms. "Very practical and cheap. Did you think I'd find out if you used regular lube? Oh, honey, you don't have to hide anything from me. And your good long, waxy candle is just the beginning. I want to get a butt plug to keep in there while I'm doing other things to you, and I want to find out how much your greedy little bum can take." Cindy whimpered with embarrassment and relief.

Shel gave her a firm slap on the bottom. "Go get your candle and oil, bad girl. And bring me a towel." Cindy went into the bedroom, and fished a plastic bag out of a drawer. Then she obediently went to the bathroom to pull a towel off the rack. She came back to Shel, and pulled a long white candle and a small bottle of vegetable oil out of the bag. She looked worried, as if she wasn't sure how to oil the candle without making a mess.

"No, don't touch that," Shel ordered. "Come lie here." She was sitting in the middle of the sofa. Trembling slightly, Cindy set the candle and oil on the coffee table and stretched herself over Shel's lap so that her bottom was in easy reach of Shel's hands.

Shel casually slid two fingers into Cindy's welcoming cunt. "Wet already," she remarked. She pulled the towel under Cindy. "I've got gloves somewhere in here," muttered Shel, reaching behind a sofa cushion. She pulled out a crumpled pair of vinyl gloves.

"Relax, babe. I want to check you out first." Shel knew that in her facedown position, Cindy needed the reassurance of Shel's voice. Shel pulled a glove onto her right hand, letting Cindy hear the snap, and squeezed a drop of oil onto her index finger. She gently spread open Cindy's anus, and slowly eased her oiled finger into the hot, tight hole. Cindy seemed to sigh all over.

"Cindy," said Shel in a low, soothing voice. "It feels so good to be in you." Shel could feel every little spasm in the delicate walls that she was gradually stretching. "I'm not hurting you, am I?"

"No-oh."

"Good." Shel was exhilarated. "I'll go in as deep as you let me." Her fingers followed the inner curve of Cindy's back passage. The phrase "carnal knowledge" took on a deeper meaning for her than it had before. The thought of touching Cindy in the guts made Shel feel like the first miner to go down a hole into the secret depths of the earth to hunt for precious minerals.

Cindy opened to Shel's spiraling finger like a flower unfolding. When Shel felt a sudden spasm of Cindy's sphincter, she distracted her by tickling her clit. "Relax," Shel told her. "It won't hurt if you let me in."

Shel's middle finger found room beside her first, and Cindy jerked in response. "Easy," Shel reminded her. "You can take it."

When Shel's two fingers were comfortably lodged in Cindy, she knew it was time to introduce the candle. "You're getting something bigger," Shel told her, "but don't come yet."

Cindy moaned when the oiled candle entered her. "Good girl," said Shel, reveling in the smooth slide of her tool into Cindy's ass. Shel felt as if she finally understood all the gay men who had ever loved this style of fucking. She felt as if she had uncovered the mystery of the smile on the faces of all the little figures in ancient Greek art.

Carefully pushing in and pulling back, Shel worked up friction that Cindy increased by moving her hips. "You like that," laughed Shel. "Wild thing. Do you need to come?"

"Shel!" Cindy answered.

"Come for me, honey," Shel told her, lightly touching her clit.

Cindy's voice rose to a wail as her anus squeezed the candle over and over while her cunt spasmed around nothing. Shel thought it better to build Cindy's desire in stages by withholding some of what she wanted at first, rather than stuffing her too full too soon.

Shel pulled the candle out gently, and noticed a few brown smears on the bottom. She was tempted to keep that candle unwashed forever as a souvenir and a delightful source of embarrassment for Cindy.

Cindy tried to move off Shel's lap, but Shel held her in place. "Are you mine?" Shel wanted to hear the answer in words.

"Oh yes. Shel, I think you're the best lover I've ever had. There's no one like you."

"You think?" was the suspicious response. "Don't you know for sure?" Shel pulled off her gloves.

Cindy squirmed under Shel's sweaty hands. "Come on, honey. I can't really remember everything I've ever done. You drove all my exes out of my mind." Cindy snickered at her own wit.

Slap! Shel's hand came down on one of Cindy's round cheeks before Shel had formed a clear plan of action. The sound, the softness of the skin on a pampered butt, and even the sting in Shel's palm intoxicated her. "Brat," she warned, trying not to laugh. "Now you'll get it."

Cindy kept squirming, but she didn't object. Shel slapped her ass again, switching from the left cheek to the right so that both would redden at the same rate.

"Ow!" yelped Cindy. But she didn't ask Shel to stop.

Shel hadn't realized how threatened she felt by Cindy's intimacy with Harv until Cindy was lying helpless under her hands. Shel believed what Cindy had told her, but she wanted to be the first one to know what Cindy was thinking and feeling. She didn't like to imagine Cindy's tête-à-têtes with her old friend, even if he was really perverse enough to prefer beefcake to feminine curves.

Slap! Slap! Shel knew that her feelings were probably selfish and unfair, but she couldn't resist giving Cindy what she seemed to be asking for. Shel wondered if they would both regret going too far.

Slap! "Oh, oh, oh," wailed Cindy. "Okay. Please. Stop."

Shel ran her hand lightly over Cindy's hot butt. "Had enough, my girl?"

"Yes. Shel, you have a hard hand."

Shel blew on Cindy's red skin to cool it, then leaned down to kiss both cheeks. Cindy giggled, moving rhythmically.

Shel reached between her legs and found her cunt incredibly wet. "But you like it," Shel pointed out. She slid two fingers deeply into Cindy's welcoming center, rubbing her clit. Violent spasms rippled though Cindy as she bucked uncontrollably, almost rolling off Shel's lap. Aside from her loud breathing, she was remarkably quiet.

Cindy wrapped her arms around Shel, pulling her into a more horizontal position. Both women shifted and slid against each other until they were pressed together, breast to breast. Shel's clothes were damp with sweat, and they felt like a ridiculous barrier between her skin and that of her honest, natural girlfriend. "Don't you want these off?" teased Cindy.

"Uh-huh," answered Shel, reluctantly easing out of Cindy's hug as Cindy tugged at her T-shirt. Shel wrestled her clothes off as if she never wanted to wear them again.

After much wiggling and laughing, Shel settled into a comfortable position on her back, holding Cindy against her. Shel ran her fingers lightly over the tender skin of the bottom she had spanked. "Honey," she told Cindy, "please don't keep secrets from me. When you have something on your mind, I'm willing to listen." Shel's blue eyes looked luminous with the pain she still felt.

"Okay." Cindy took in a deep, comforting breath and let it out. "I won't keep secrets from you, Shel." She pressed her lips to Shel's. "I don't want to hurt you." Cindy sounded sincere, but she couldn't keep the brattiness out of her voice for long. "No shit."

Shel snickered. "Honesty," she responded, "is the bottom line in a good relationship." Both women laughed until all their cheeks shook.

THE CAPTAIN'S WALK

Dominic Santi

The house on State Street was haunted. The sign outside the small historical museum on the first floor said the captain of the *Madelaine* had gone down with his ship in a raging gale on Lake Michigan one hundred and fifty years before. His ghost had returned to the three-story mansion he'd called his "other home." By the time The Captain's Walk unexpectedly came to me, it had long ago been designated an official tourist attraction—the second floor and most of the third turned into a much-sought-after bed and breakfast.

I was pleased to learn gossip about the ghost's visits kept the guest quarters booked solid, six months in advance. I'd inherited the house from my godfather, who'd inherited it from his godfather, who'd inherited it from his, and so on in an unbroken chain of unmarried men, all the way back to the twenty-three-year-old cabin boy to whom the captain had originally bequeathed the house. When I'd signed the papers agreeing to the will's stipulation to keep the third floor lakefront apartment for my own quarters, including the "haunted" walkway around the gables, I told the executor in no uncertain terms that I didn't believe in ghosts. I had a brand-new degree in marketing and hotel management. In the weeks leading up to Halloween, the traditional time for the restless captain to make his presence known, I was going to capitalize on the lucrative paranormal angles that brought in the annual busloads of museum visitors in addition to the overnight guests. But I, personally, didn't believe in ghosts.

The day after I moved in, I told the museum director that I didn't believe in doors slamming in vacant rooms or floating panpipes playing bawdy tunes in the parlor or objects being translocated from one display case to another after hours. If he was unable to keep his precious, newly discovered artifacts from the *Madelaine* where they belonged, he should hire a security guard to work the night shift for the rest of the month. A week later, I reassured my third-floor guests that the rattling windows and the shadows dancing in the decorative rum bottles were caused by leaves blowing past their windows. Then I reassured my second-floor guests that their rooms were every bit as good as those on the third floor.

The Saturday evening before the High Holy Day of the thirty-first, I told the dozen close friends I'd invited to a private party in the museum's social hall that with another couple years of cretins buying into the whole ridiculous haunted house scenario, I was going to be a millionaire before I was thirty.

"Are you sure he's not real?" my friend, Raymond, simpered as he twirled a handblown crystal wineglass stem in his fingers. He was gazing up at the larger-than-life-sized portrait of the captain gracing the entryway. The head above the uniformed shoulders stared down reprovingly at us. "Your cutie pie captain could haunt me anytime. Icy gray eyes. Long black hair with just

enough silver to let you know he's been around. And those shoulders!" Raymond shivered dramatically. "Honey, you just know
he'd hold you down and fuck you till you shot all over your chin!"

Raymond took a deep drink of his wine. "Too bad we can't
see the rest of him. I bet he had a basket big enough to make
your mouth water." He lifted his glass toward the picture on the
opposite wall. "He'd have been after your ass in no time, sweet
cheeks. You look just like his 'cabin boy' there. I'd bet a large
portion of my stock portfolio what led our dear departed captain
to leave his entire estate to that one. You'll notice *his* portrait is
a full body pose—in profile, so one can see the luscious curve of
his exceptionally fine ass." Raymond turned me sideways and
leered. "Coincidence? I think not!"

I had to agree that I looked like the cabin boy. We shared the
same short, slender build, the same straight blond hair that fell into
our eyes—hazel eyes. But my ass was definitely sexier. I deter-
minedly steered Raymond back to the open bar for which my
first two months' receipts were paying.

Raymond was all about noticing men's asses. Especially
mine, though these days I was so busy with the mansion I didn't
have much time for entertaining. Most nights, I fell into bed, too
exhausted to even masturbate. And for some insane reason, I was
having wet dreams again, damn near every night. I told myself
it was my lack of sex life that had me dreaming that the cabin
boy's ass had rebelled as much as mine did when a cock tried to
intrude, or that my too-tight hole pissed the captain off as much
as his original cabin boy's had well over a century before.

All the way up to Halloween, I told everybody I knew that
while ghosts were good for business, I didn't believe in them.
Never had, never would.

Then I shut the fuck up. Because I didn't want to tell anybody that no matter how I felt about ghosts in general, I sure as

fuck believed in the big wooden peg stretching my asshole open every night as I sat back on the cabin boy's wooden chair. As the grandfather clock in the hall had struck midnight on Halloween, my terrified yelps had been lost in the noise as I'd danced to the icy hot bursts of angry energy the captain's ghost shot across my naked ass.

As the echoes of the clock had died away, I'd fumbled the attic door open and scurried up the stairs ahead of the captain. I'd retrieved the dusty trunk I only vaguely remembered seeing under the eaves, and hauled it back down the stairs and through the open door as the captain glided through the walls beside me. Then, with the captain still muttering about idiots who didn't believe their own eyes, I'd put the trunk down by the bed and obediently lifted the lid.

Inside was an assortment of the captain's personal belongings: shirts and trousers and a leather vest that still held the faint scent of salt spray and masculine sweat. A heavy woolen coat lay on the bottom, beneath a half-dozen leather books, a small silver flute, and a wooden chest for which there seemed to be no key. At the captain's direction, I took out an exquisite cobalt blue bottle. When I worked the stopper free, a drop of the slipperiest oil I'd ever felt spilled onto my finger. Still too stunned to speak, I wiped my hand on my leg and picked up a heavy swatch of purple velvet.

Inside lay a sturdy wooden peg shaped remarkably like an extra-large butt plug. A sudden cold wind blew through the wall and tossed the cushion from the straight-backed chair I'd placed in front of the window the day I'd moved in. There, in the middle of the polished wooden seat, was a small, round hole—a hole that exactly matched the metal screw on the bottom of the peg.

Three weeks later, I was used to waking naked in what I now knew were the captain's rooms. I was used to respectfully stripping from the waist down the moment I stepped through his door each night. And after three weeks of lubing the peg and my ass with oil from the captain's bottle and squatting back over what I now thought of as "my" chair, I was convinced to my bones that not only did ghosts exist, they were every bit as horny as their full-bodied counterparts.

"Your asshole is a disgrace," the captain snapped, leaning back against the hand-painted silk wallpaper of our bedroom. "Lower yourself slowly. Stop when it hurts."

"Yes, sir," I whispered, trying not to notice how the end of his filmy white elbow sank into the wall. No matter how often I fucked myself on the peg, I'd never been able to take it all. It was nowhere near the size of the huge mound of flesh swelling the front of the captain's impeccable uniform trousers. It wasn't even as big as my own modestly sized dick, which now hung limply between my legs. I wanted to be fucked, but my ass just wouldn't cooperate.

The small rounded tip pressed pleasantly at my back gate. As usual, the first little bit felt good, almost like a lover's finger sliding in. Not that any of my lovers, even Raymond, had known jack shit about easing my perpetually too-tight asshole open. As the peg flared wider, the gentle friction turned swiftly to stretching, then to burn. I exhaled hard, bearing down, willing my ass to relax.

"Ow!" I hissed as my muscles clenched painfully.

"Up." The captain's voice wasn't loud, but I obeyed instantly. The electricity searing across my butt on Halloween night had left me too sore to sit down for days, despite the absolute absence of any marks on my skin. But I had to admit, that wasn't my main incentive. After three weeks of draining my balls nightly in the most glorious orgasms of my life, just the sound of the captain's voice was the best aphrodisiac I'd ever known. I sighed with relief as the width of the peg diminished.

"Stop."

I froze, my leg muscles tightening as I paused in mid-squat. The tip of the peg just barely teased inside my sphincters. They fluttered against the slippery wood, kissing it in reflex until my cock stirred at the stimulation. The captain pulled his pipe out of his pocket, filling the bowl and tamping down the tobacco. As my legs strained to hold my weight, he turned and struck a wooden match on a fireplace brick. The flame flared a ghostly bluish white. I braced my hands against my knees, holding myself still over the chair. My asslips now kissed the peg in earnest, reaching hungrily for more. The captain touched the match to his pipe, smiling contentedly as tendrils of smoke rose from the meerschaum bowl.

"Down."

I slowly lowered myself, my legs straining as my sphincters stretched over the peg. Smoke wafted past me and my nose twitched, searching for a whiff of sweet tobacco. Nothing came but the ever-present smell of pine and the spicy scent of the captain's oil. As the tendrils passed into the far wall, the pleasant stretch again turned to burn. I winced.

"Up, dammit!"

A bolt of ice snapped across my ass. I yelped, gingerly rubbing my right cheek as I quickly raised myself. I froze again at the growled, "Stop! In my day, I'd have bent you over a rail and laid a cat to your ass." Blue-white electricity quivered in the hand not holding the pipe. "The peg boy's hole should be ready to service the captain's cock, any time, day or night!" He snapped his fingers and another line of icy fire cracked across my butt. I hissed as my sphincters once more trembled fiercely around the stiff wooden tip.

"I want that hole loose and slippery, boy, any time I choose to take it! You've got a long way to go!" He shook his head in disgust, tapping his ashes into the fireplace. A small puff of vaporous dust rose from the hearth. He looked back at me sternly.

"Don't just stand there! Lube your peg again and start over!"

I stretched my legs, working out the knots as I hurriedly dripped lube on the huge, shiny wooden peg. Despite my hole's rebelliousness, it felt suddenly empty without the peg. I smiled when I lowered myself and the slippery wood once more stretched my asslips.

"Feels good, aye, boy?"

I looked up to see him smiling at me. The pipe was back in his pocket.

"Yes, sir," I blushed, this time slowing on my own as the pleasure stretched to pain. The peg was in deeper now. I braced my hands on my thighs.

"Stop."

Again, I froze. The captain was kneading his crotch. Even through the straining wool, his dick was impressive, swelling to almost the size of my wrist.

"Squeeze. Release. Squeeze." His hand matched his commands. "Work your hole, boy."

My hole was obeying all on its own. Squeeze, release. Squeeze, release. My eyes stayed glued to the big, calloused hand pumping the shimmering bulge. A dark spot was forming at the tip. Bracing one hand on my knee, I grabbed my own soft cock, tugging as the warm flesh filled and grew heavy. All my life, I'd dreamed of taking a cock like his up my ass. I'd dreamed of being stretched so wide and fucked so hard I'd feel the come being pressed out of my balls. Dreamed I'd feel hot pre-come leaking through my dick, lubing my palm as I stroked and twisted.

I kept my eyes glued to the captain's crotch, dreaming of a fuck that would let me take his thick, throbbing cock all the way up my hole. A stretch that would mean he was fucking me and fucking me....

I gasped as my asslips gave way. My buttcheeks touched wood, and the peg pressed into my prostate. I threw my head back, howling as hot jism pulsed through my quaking cock and into my hand. I shook on my peg, coming and coming as the dark spot spread on the front of the captain's pants. My ears echoed with the sound of his deep, rumbling laughter as the smell of my own musky juice filled the air.

I slumped forward in my chair, trailing my fingers through the sticky puddle cooling on my belly as my breathing finally slowed.

"Ah, boy. What I'd give to taste a cabin boy's spunk again." His hand was contentedly kneading the wet spot in his own now considerably less swollen crotch. "Slippery and salty..."

"Enough to make your mouth water." I grinned up at him. The captain winked.

"A well-drained cock goes with a good, hard fuck, boy." He walked through the table toward me. I closed my eyes as a soft wind brushed against my skin. I still couldn't make myself watch when his fingers moved through me, but at last I no longer flinched. Peaceful, cool tingles flowed through me, then a single icy jolt shot suddenly up my spine. I gasped as a last drop of semen oozed through my cockhead and my ass-hole once more spasmed ferociously over the peg. The captain chuckled.

"When the clock strikes one, go to bed. Leave the chair where it is. And sleep on your side or your belly. I may want to take your ass again when I'm done dealing with the historical society idiots."

"Yes, sir!" I said, even though I knew he was gone. I spent the next few minutes watching the night sky out the window, wishing I'd taken the time to learn the constellations. The room felt cooler now. Goose bumps shivered up my back and the peg felt suddenly huge. I squeezed it uncomfortably, rubbing my hands over my arms.

White flames burst from the dry logs lying stacked but unlit in the fireplace. I knew the fire wasn't real. But as the room heated just enough to keep me comfortable, I wiggled on the chair, enjoying the warmth and the totally well-fucked and worn-out feeling in my tired, contented ass. When the clock struck one, I stood up. My asshole was sore, but I was too tired to care. I climbed between the covers and was asleep as my head hit the pillow.

I dreamed erotic dreams. Wild, color-filled dreams, the kind I'd had only since I moved into the captain's house. Strong, rough hands pinched my nips. A fiery cold tongue licked slowly up my cock, poking imperiously into my piss slit. Cool soothing lube spurted up my ass, soothing away the irritation and pleasuring my joyspot until my cock once more spurted onto my belly. I woke facedown with my cock stuck to the sheets and an icy lash searing across my ass.

"OW!" I twisted around, yanking the covers back up. They jerked out of my hands, pulling me forward in a tangle of blankets. I lost my balance, my legs falling to the floor as I was bent conveniently over the edge of the bed.

"Ow. Ow! OW!" Icy cracks blazed painfully over my ass as I howled and twisted in the covers.

"I should whip you till you can't walk, you idiot!" The captain roared, lacing the backs of my thighs with a flurry of stokes before he once more whipped up and down my ass. As the sheets released me, I scrambled to my feet, grabbing my butt, tears streaming down my face. I tried in vain to squeeze away the fire I felt only in my ass, not on my hands.

"I'm sorry, sir!" I sobbed, arching forward as a blast of cold air jerked me around to face him. I stared up into his furious face. "What did I do, sir?"

The captain pointed wordlessly toward the chair, still sitting where I'd left it the night before in front of the window. Morning sun glistened on the gleaming surface. Even through my tears, I could see the dark red spot on the side of the peg.

"If you EVER feel real pain again, you WILL tell me immediately!" The air crackled blue fire around his fingers as he threw a bolt of energy at the chair. I backed up against the bed, shaking as the peg exploded in a shower of silvery wooden splinters. "Do you understand me, boy?!"

"Yes, sir!" I nodded so hard my head bobbled, gaping at the shattered remnants of the peg. The captain jerked his head toward the door and snarled. "Get downstairs to your guests. The tone-deaf woman from 2C is having the vapors because she heard pipes playing last night. And the museum director is in an uproar because that worthless sextant those fools dragged from the wreck of the *Madelaine* is suddenly in the women's lingerie case rather than with the rest of the navigational instruments. Fool. If the damn sextant had worked, the ship wouldn't have gone down!"

Another crackle singed the air beside me, but it flew past my butt and halfheartedly ruffled the sheets. Leaving the bed unmade, I dragged on my clothes and raced out of the room.

The next week was spent in a flurry of customer relations. I smoothed the ruffled feathers of those who had heard furniture moving and howling cries in the night—and of those who were disappointed they hadn't. Rumors of another "appearance" by the ghost caused a rush of out-of-town tourists and local folks once again lined up for museum tours. By the time I dragged myself up to our rooms at night, I was too tired for anything but a quick game of chess with the captain before I crawled into bed.

At his direction, I'd cleaned up the shattered remnants of the peg and moved the chair to the table at which I sat, facing him, for our games. It felt strange wiggling my naked butt against the pegless chair while we each moved both sets of pieces on our matching boards. I yawned, leaning forward to rest my face on my sleeve as I fingered the nick in the bishop's miter and waited for the captain to move.

"You carved this whole set yourself, sir?" The wood was smooth and warm. It was comforting to touch something the captain had physically held, even though he'd done it long before I was born.

"A man at sea has a great deal of time on his hands. Check."

I took one look at the board and, with a sigh, tipped over my king. Then I stretched my arms high over my head. "I'm getting pretty sleepy, sir. Another game tomorrow night?"

The captain's laugh was low and throaty. I glanced at him, my cock stirring unexpectedly. He laughed even harder, kneading his crotch as he stood up and nodded toward my bed.

"Get some sleep, boy. We'll play tomorrow night."

With another bone-jarring yawn, I nodded, peeled off my shirt, and once more climbed naked between the sheets.

Again, I dreamed cool, wet, sexy dreams. My asshole tingled. But instead of waking stuck to the sheets, I woke with a raging hard-on and guests clamoring for breakfast. All day, my hands wandered to my crotch as I thought about the captain's cock. By the time I'd turned the *closed* sign on the museum door and the guests were all safely ensconced in the parlor with spiked cider, I was so horny I climbed the stairs two at a time.

"Not yet," the captain said gruffly as I reached for my belt buckle. I turned to see him sitting in the easy chair on the far side of the room, one foot on the ottoman and an arm resting half in the side of the armoire. Instead of his usual impeccable uniform, he was wearing rough seaman's clothes: loose trousers and a long-sleeved white shirt, and high, shining leather boots. A single silver hoop shimmered in his left ear. His hair was tied back in a loose leather thong. The front of his shirt was open, revealing a thick forest of frosty hair on rippling pecs. I licked my lips. His crotch was swollen, a single dark spot dampening the tip where his cockhead pressed into the straining fabric. The captain chuckled softly.

"Inside the trunk, on the bottom right side, you'll find a small panel hidden immediately behind the front corner. Press in and up."

I carefully lifted the books and clothes from the trunk, pressing my face for a moment to the vest that still held the faint hint of my captain's scent. The panel opened easily to my touch. I took out a small, silver key.

"Unlock the chest."

For a moment, visions of gold and jewels filled my head. And for the entire length of that moment, I resented that treasure to the core of my being for interfering with my time with the captain. I looked up, frowning at his uproarious laughter.

"What...sir?"

"You have a one-track mind, boy. Which delights me no end." He moved his fingers like he was turning a key. "And luckily for you, you remembered your manners. Go on."

With a click, the lock popped open. I lifted the lid. My mouth went dry. Resting on a bed of shimmering black silk was a huge ivory phallus. It was bigger than the peg had been. Bigger than any cock I'd ever seen. It was smooth and perfectly detailed, down to the bulging veins and the wrinkled skin where the cowl had been pushed back by the straining head. I knew without looking whose cock had been the model.

"You know what to do."

I nodded, swallowing hard. A thick metal screw protruded from the bottom of the shaft. A moment later, the phallic peg was jutting up in all its majesty from the seat of my chair. I ran my fingers over the smooth, almost glowing surface. After all the times I'd lusted for my captain's cock, my fingers couldn't get enough of touching the pure ivory replica.

"You have a beautiful cock, sir." I looked up, stunned to see him unbuttoning his pants. For all the times I'd been naked in front of him, he'd never removed his clothes in my presence.

"Strip, boy." The front of his pants fell open. His cock fell out into his hand. It was long and thick, every detail exactly like that of its perfect replica. He stroked himself, his leaking head winking in and out of its cover. "Get the oil."

"Yes, sir!" My hands shook as I threw my clothes on the floor. I grabbed the cobalt bottle from the nightstand, dripping oil on my fingers. The captain's growl was low and mean.

"If you'd made a mess like that in my cabin, I'd have whipped your ass with your own belt before I fucked you!"

"Yes, sir." I blushed, sweeping my clothes off the floor with one hand and tossing them over the trunk. I smeared oil over the phallus, letting the slippery lube drip down onto the wooden seat as I squatted back and greased my asshole. I wasn't sore at all anymore. In fact, my hole itched to be filled. I petted it a few more times before I set the oil back on the stand. I turned to face him. "Should I straddle the chair, S—?"

My voice died away as I stared at my captain's fully naked body. Although I'd always sensed the physical strength beneath his clothes, I was stunned at the pure, masculine power still lingering in the hazy echoes of his work-toned flesh. Every moment of the backbreaking manual labor he'd done to captain his ship showed in the wiry, rippling muscles of his arms and legs and torso. His scrotum hung low and heavy beneath his fully engorged cock. He tugged his balls with one hand, stroking his shaft with the other as he stared purposefully at the perfect ivory phallus.

"Spread your cheeks with both hands, boy. Lower yourself until the tip is against your hole."

I nodded, not trusting myself to speak. I straddled the chair and slowly squatted back. When the smooth knob touched my sphincter, I stopped.

"Press just enough to make it stretch," the captain said. "Then stop!"

I nodded vigorously, squatting until my hole kissed open-mouthed and greedy against the slippery ivory head. At some very primal level, my body wasn't afraid anymore. I'd taken the widest part of the wooden peg. I hadn't been sufficiently care-ful, but I now knew my hole could stretch enough to take a real man's cock. My ass was hungry and horny and ready to be fucked.

"Touch yourself." The captain ran his hands up his arms, sliding over his chest and down his torso. He circled his heart and belly and cradled his crotch before sliding back up to caress his neck and chin. Then his hands moved over his arms again. I released my bottom cheeks, my asshole suddenly intensely aware of the large, smooth tip pressing straight into the middle of my sphincter.

My legs burned, but my hands felt good on my skin. I matched my strokes to the captain's, constantly aware of the pressure in my ass. My skin came alive under my hands, my hole opening slowly like a mouth parting for a deep tongue thrust. The ivory cock was sliding in, the warm relentless pressure easing my asslips wider. I gasped, arching forward as the head slid through.

"Don't," the captain said quietly. His hands circled his heart and abs before they once more slid down to stroke his crotch. I breathed in deeply, letting the air out slowly, willing my ass not to tighten as I matched my movements to his. Up, over, around. I shivered into my hands as my ass stretched slowly down the shaft of the huge phallic spear.

"Does it hurt, boy?"

"No, sir," I panted, realizing as I spoke that while the phallus kissed right up next to hurting, it was still my captain's cock. I wanted it so badly, and it felt so good. I gasped as it slid deeper.

"Easy." The captain moved toward me, his fingers caressing his cock. A web of pre-come dripped from his fingertips. This time, I didn't close my eyes. A chill like champagne bubbles sparkled over my skin as he stroked his hand down my arm. I smiled at him, leaning back, the phallus sliding deeper as his fingers pressed into my wrist. Cool liquid electricity pulsed through my veins. My legs burned holding my weight as the captain's other hand circled my chest, his fingers tingling down over my cock, sliding through my leg to stroke me behind my balls.

"I'm going to fuck you now, boy." The captain eased around my shoulder, the chill of his torso sliding through my side as he moved in back of me. A film, like icy lube, slid over the phallus. I cried out, closing my eyes, my ass opening in one long, burning stretch as I lowered myself onto the chair. Cool pressure rocked up into me, into a place that made my dick leak and my hole relax with pleasure. I shivered as a trail of kisses traveled up my neck.

"Up and down, boy. Ride your captain's cock."

I braced my hands on my thighs, fucking myself over the captain's cock. The delicious, icy friction seared through me until my arms and legs shook and my skin crawled with lust. I wanted my captain in me. I wanted him filling me and fucking me, until every nerve in my body was his. The sounds coming from my mouth weren't words anymore, just soft keening cries as the captain's laughter vibrated through me.

"Stroke yourself."

I grabbed my throbbing cock. The contrast of heat from my hand and the coolness of the captain's shaft left me trembling. My ass squeezed around him, instinctive, rhythmic clenching that was completely beyond my control. With each squeeze, clear hot juice leaked from my cockhead. Each time the captain's cock slid into me, I wanted to scream with pleasure.

"I'm going to come, sir." I forced myself to form the words as my body once more shuddered around his.

"I can feel your heat, boy," the captain whispered. A chill passed through me as his arms came up to pinch my nipples. My hole was so loose I was riding him freely now. My body drew in on itself, my cock stretching out stiff and hard into my hand as the captain pounded my joyspot.

"Now!"

Icy waves flooded my ass. I bucked back in the chair, howling as my orgasm exploded through me. Liquid heat pulsed through my shaft and I rocked onto the captain's body, screaming as a jolt of pure, molten bliss seared up my spine. The solid wholeness of his body cradled me in his arms while pleasure and pain and need became one, until they were everything. I reached for the brilliant light chiming in front of me, laughing as I stretched my asshole as wide as I could, taking my lover into me as my cock emptied into my hand.

"Not yet, laddie," the captain panted softly in my ear. In a surge of ice, I was alone. The captain leaned once more into the wall, smiling sadly as he tucked his now come-covered cock back into his pants. My legs were still quaking, but I rose shakily from the chair. Tears streamed down my face. I didn't bother wiping them away. I just looked into my captain's glittering gray eyes and fell back onto the bed.

"I don't understand, sir. But thank you." I snuggled into the covers, shivering as the sheets warmed to my skin. I was fading rapidly into sleep.

The captain's voice was warm and soothing. "You'll understand someday, my boy. For now, you've earned your rest, as you've earned the right to sit on the peg boy's chair and enjoy our games of chess every night. I'll wait until you're asleep to haunt the guests tonight."

I dreamed someone was screaming about panpipes, but I didn't bother waking up. They'd paid to be scared, and meeting ghosts wasn't painless. If anything was truly wrong, my captain would wake me. I was content to sleep in the echoes of his love.

ROOM SERVICE

N. T. Morley

"Do you think you could fit it in my ass?" she asked, breathlessly, sprawled on the bed in her bikini, legs spread, hair mussed, as the wind whistled in from the open French doors facing the beach.

Her hair was mussed from the wind, not because we'd been making love—which we hadn't, for probably the first three-hour period since we'd arrived in Panama. Even on the short Copa flight from Panama City to David, there was the soft blanket she'd packed to cover us, her hand finding my cock underneath and stroking me hard through my jeans. Even on the drive from David to the seaside resort of Las Olas on the Golfo de Chiriqui, she'd snuggled up and whispered dirty things into my ear, begging me to finger her. Our first day in the hotel room was spent in bed, a blur of sex and room service, embarrassed waiters eyeing the ravaged bedclothes while Jolie hid in the bathroom for just long enough for them to set the table, housekeeping knocking with increasing perturbation and more frenzied cries of

"*¿Hojas neuvas?*" throughout the day as we soiled and resoiled and re-resoiled those luxurious three-hundred-thread-count sheets into a tangled, sweaty, festering mass, testament to our shamelessness, or something.

That we'd joined the Mile-High Club on the flight down from LAX—or, rather, that Jolie had joined, me already being a charter member—was just further evidence of how swiftly she was adapting to her new chosen role in life.

She'd divorced, recently—or was in the process of divorcing—a guy who apparently thought twice-monthly sex was more than enough. At twenty-six, she was both a fresh divorcee and an astonishingly submissive slut. That her sexual adventures before her divorce had been limited to one abortive college-era threesome, a lukewarm bondage session with silk scarves, about fifteen minutes in bed during which she called her then-boyfriend Master (which made him freak out and suggest that they attend couples therapy), and, more recently, a furtive attempt to cheat on her husband with the pizza delivery boy (which is another story, and one so sad even I can't bear to tell it), only made her more able, now that she had a dirty old man like me, to fulfill both stereotypical female roles at once—she was simultaneously a virgin and a slut.

She was a whole lot better at being a slut.

But even so, her lack of experience often emboldened her, bolstered her confidence, made her ask for things like this, savage and terrifying in her hunger, enthusiastic in her risk taking, utterly unclear on the sorts of things that even sluts—even the horniest, most oversexed, most adventurous sluts—generally asked for.

Because she wasn't talking about my cock.

No, I had already had the pleasure of taking the submissive Jolie's ass for the first time, telling her—at her suggestion—that all submissive sluts had to take it in the ass. I had already fucked her quite soundly in her behind, even double-penetrated her, the thickness of a hefty silicone dildo filling her pussy as I entered her ass and felt the hard material pressing through Jolie and against me, making her rear entry even tighter than before. That particular incident, three weeks ago to the day, was when Jolie found out she could squirt.

Since then, she liked it anally as often as she liked it the other way. I had fucked her back door with my cock, my tongue; with fingers, with anal beads and dildos—some of which were considerably larger than my cock and, to be fair, not all that much smaller than my hand. I had all but created a monster, but then she was a very pretty monster, looking beautiful in her string bikini and spread most deliciously across the king-sized bed.

And introducing Jolie to the pleasures of backdoor love was far from my only privilege with her. I had also fisted her, two weeks ago to the day, my hand finally sliding into her pussy after a marathon session of four fingers, no thumb, said thumb's long-awaited insertion bringing a bestial yowl from her lips as she added streams of her recently discovered ejaculate to the slippery gumbo of lube and pussy that coated my arm up to the elbow—and most of my chest, now that you mentioned it.

How natural, then, that within twenty-four hours of arriving in Chiriqui, Jolie should seek to combine those two pleasures, asking such an impertinent question: "Your hand, I mean. Do you think you could fit it up my *ass*?"

That word, *ass*, positively dripped with a filthy sexual liquor as it passed her lips. I fully believe it sounded more sullied and erotic than the word ever has before. That she whispered softly afterward, almost too quietly for me to hear, "my tight…little… asshole?" only added to the filth of the whole thing. And my cock was so hard, so fast, that the three hours we'd spent without me inside her or our mouths and/or bodies pressed together seemed like an eternity.

"I've got pretty big hands," I told her, as she traced one fingertip with her tongue, nibbling on it.

"I know," she whispered as her tongue slid its way down my palm and she began to swirl it in a circle at the underside of my wrist. "That's what makes it so exciting. I took you once before," she said.

"A lot more than once," I grumbled, as she nibbled at the soft flesh of my forearm.

"Three times in two weeks," she said. "I'm a fisting slut. You *made* me a fisting slut, lover. The least you can do is finish the job."

She lingered with her lips at the heel of my hand, her eyes sparkling with mischief, and looked at me hungrily.

"Debauch me utterly," she begged me. "Put your fist in my ass."

"Oh," I said with a frown. "You think *that* will debauch you utterly?"

She gave a strangely girlish giggle, and I swear I saw her color deepen just a bit.

"Until you find something even filthier to do to me," she whispered.

Jolie had a deeply submissive side, which came out clearly despite her aggressive pursuit of more and better perversions. It was always me "doing" things to her, even when it was her idea, even when she begged for it. I certainly had lots of things I could do to her—but even with the most submissive girlfriend I could have imagined, I wouldn't have anticipated sliding my fist into her ass six weeks after our first meeting.

Jolie, however, was in a class by herself.

"There are many things filthier," I said, my voice a low, care-fully modulated grumble, "much, much filthier than having my fist in your ass."

She shivered.

"I know," she said. "But this is pretty filthy."

She was stretched on the bed, legs spread, ass entirely revealed except for the thin string that formed the back of her spandex thong. My hand found her ass and touched it, and a shudder went through her as if she'd been touched by a live wire. Without further preliminaries, I plucked her thong out of the way and slid two fingers into her pussy. She was so far beyond wet that any reticence I'd felt vanished with the feeling of her tight entrance gripping my fingers. My thumb touched her ass-hole and nuzzled it firmly. She moaned.

"First things first," I said. "We should clean you out."

She flushed ever-so-slightly deeper, and gave me the shy look that was half virgin, half tease, and all slut.

"I'm very, very dirty," she whispered.

I stripped her down quickly, climbing on top of her so she could feel the pressure of my cock against the small of her back, stretching through the swimsuit I wore. I forced her legs together and took the thong off over her ankles, tossing it carelessly on the floor. Reversing my position, I guided her into a sitting position, slapped her hand away from the tie at her neck as she tried to unfasten it. She obediently put her arms at her sides in a submissive posture. I tugged at the knot and it gave way. The red bikini top—barely there to begin with—fell forward, revealing Jolie's perfect tits, nipples hard from arousal.

I had done it that way because I wanted to see them. I wanted to see her nipples, hard, ready, just another indicator of how much she wanted this. But, seeing them, seeing the pride and the heat on her face, I could not resist one of the other things I loved so much about her—those lips.

They were painted bright red, so inappropriate for sunbathing. But Jolie, the born-again slut, never went anywhere without her lips stained cocksucker red. I pulled down my swimsuit and snapped my fingers.

Her mouth was on my cock in an instant, lavishing it with affection, her tongue swirling around my head before her head sank forward until her lips met the base of my cock. She had only learned to deep-throat recently. But she did it like an expert.

As she sucked me, I reached down and pulled the bikini top the rest of the way off, balled it up and tossed it into the corner.

The French doors to the balcony were open; I knew it and Jolie knew it. If she hadn't already been as wet as a human female could possibly be, this awareness would have made her wetter. The balcony faced the gulf; the chances of someone seeing us were slim. It would require one of those boaters out there to have a telescope and perfect aim. But that mattered little to Jolie, who loved to think that people might see her at such a moment.

"Spread your legs," I told her.

She did, and I pushed her back onto the bed, entering her in one smooth thrust.

She cried out and arched her back, pushing her breasts against me. I kissed her, hard, tasting my own cock and feeling her tongue surge against mine. A few thrusts was all it took to leave her gasping and moaning as I withdrew and stood up again, pulling her into a sitting position and guiding her mouth back to my cock. The smear of lipstick made her lips look like they'd been turned about fifteen degrees to one side. The sight of it made me harder than ever.

She swallowed more eagerly this time, her arousal evident as her already impressive skills improved. I had to pull her off me, my hand tangled in her hair.

I tucked my cock away and straightened my swimsuit.

"Get in the bathtub," I told her, conjuring the rough growl that always made her hungry. "Bent over the edge."

"Yes, Sir," said Jolie, and hurried naked into the bathroom, wiping her moistened lips.

I thanked our lucky stars that the suitcase with the enema nozzle hadn't been the one the screener had opened at LAX. The six containers of lube had embarrassed the poor girl enough. The rubber end of the tube was designed to fit onto any bathtub faucet; the coiled chrome hose was like a serpent waiting to strike. Its lone fang was a bullet-shaped silver nozzle, ten inches long, smooth as a rocket. I carried it and the small travel kit packed with nothing but lubricant into the bathroom.

Jolie was already positioned in the deeply-sunken bathtub, bent at the waist, her upper body stretched around the floor while her legs stretched out into the empty tub. We'd already discovered that with a sunken tub such as this one, that was the most comfortable position to make her accessible from behind for a lengthy period. Her legs were spread and her hips gently rocked back and forth, the scent of her arousal so strong it met my nostrils before I even approached her.

One end fit tightly over the faucet. Jolie shut her eyes and took deep breaths as I turned on the water, felt the gentle stream against my wrist to make sure it was the right temperature—warm, but not hot. She had never had an enema before; it had been one of the pleasures—or is that humiliations?—I'd promised her on this trip, but I'd never thought it would be in preparation for a fisting.

But she was ready—positioned, dripping wet, her asshole awakened by the knowledge of what was to come. I turned off the water. I opened the lube and squeezed out a healthy quantity.

I did not, however, apply it to fingers or nozzle. There are more pleasurable ways to lubricate a beautiful woman's asshole, especially when she's bent over, completely accessible, desperately horny, and deeply submissive.

I pulled down my swimsuit again, applied the lube to my cock. Jolie's eyes were still shut tightly, her breath coming short. I entered her without warning, feeling the tightness of her asshole clench and give way against the head of my cock. I went deep into her, her mewling cry as I penetrated her urging me on. I withdrew my cock, applied more lube, and slid my cock in deep again.

I could have come; I was very close already. I longed to deposit my seed in that tight hole of Jolie's, to feel her milk me dry. But I wouldn't have dreamed of cheating Jolie or me of the extra cruelty and pleasure I would show if I was right on the edge, and desperate to come.

I withdrew my cock five more times and slid it in four, applying lube with each reentry, each time coaxing a cry of pleasure from Jolie's mouth. She was lubed well and deep, her anus glistening with the thick gel. When I could hold back no more, I put my cock away, breathing deeply. Then I gently parted Jolie's cheeks with my hands and inserted the nozzle slowly.

I had to go slower than I could with my cock—the nozzle was, after all, made of metal. But I went no less deep—in fact, given ten inches to work with, I filled her up quite efficiently, gently nuzzling my way against the first curve. I turned on the faucet, very low, and watched Jolie's body stiffen as warm water began to fill her up.

A bag would have been more ideal, in some ways, because it allowed one to measure the amount of water being delivered.

But this would have to do for now. I knew that Jolie, being petite, would have to be watched carefully so I could tell when she was full. I knew that something in her eyes would tell me.

"Wow," I heard her say.

"Lift your belly off the edge of the tub," I ordered, and she did it with some difficulty. It wouldn't do to have pressure against her lower belly as she was filled. She braced herself against the edge of the tub. With the position her head was in now, I couldn't resist.

I came around and slid my cock into her mouth. She sucked me hungrily as she felt her colon swelling with the warm liquid.

A few strokes of her mouth was all it would have taken. I allowed her one less than necessary. I drew my cock out of her mouth and held back my orgasm with great difficulty. I climbed into the tub and reached under Jolie's body to feel how swollen her lower belly was.

She gasped.

"You're nice and full," I said. "Think you can take more?"

"I—I don't know," she whimpered. "Sir."

That told me she could take more, and I took a moment to slide two fingers into her pussy, feeling the tightness caused by the insertion of the nozzle. I rubbed her clit. She moaned as she was filled.

It was guesswork, to know when the pressure was too much. But I must have made a very good guess, because as I switched off the tap and slowly withdrew the nozzle, she gave a little yelp and a tiny glop of clean water escaped.

She began to climb out of the tub.

"No!" I said firmly. "Stay here."

She turned miserably to face me, her eyes crazy with the pressure inside her. I drew her close to me and kissed her deeply, her tongue feeling thick with desperation. I reached around to cup her buttocks, feeling them tensed and tight.

"Do you feel full?" I asked her.

"Yes, Sir," she said, and I knew I'd pushed her to that point where her arousal matched her fear, matched her humiliation, matched her need to stop. But she had a safeword, and she had used it before. I knew, if she needed, she would use it again.

"Lean back against the edge of the tub," I told her.

It chagrined me slightly to have to slide a condom on—Jolie and I did not use them except in situations like this, neither of us having fucked another living soul for longer than the period covered by our tests. But tucked in the lube-filled travel kit, alongside the watertight baggie of gloves, there were two strips of six condoms. There had been some discussion—would be more discussion, I was quite sure, before our week in Chiriqui was finished—of finding a man for Jolie to fuck on my orders.

Before that would happen, however, at least one condom would be put to good use.

I opened the package and popped the condom into Jolie's mouth. She obediently lowered herself to her knees, whimpering with the discomfort inside her, and rolled the rubber sheath onto my cock with her mouth. She was shaking by the time she got it on me.

"Do you remember it?"

"Yes, Sir," she said.

"Do you want to use it?"

"More than anything," she whimpered. "But I won't. Sir."

I pushed her back against the edge of the tub, her sudden wail of inner distension music to my ears as I entered her almost painfully tight pussy. She clutched herself to me and winced, gritting her teeth between moans of discomfort. I fucked her there against the edge of the tub, feeling all her muscles cinched so tight that before long I suspected she would *have* to release them, whether she wanted to or not.

I toyed with the idea of making her reach that point—the very thought of it was enough to make me let go and come. But I didn't, on either count. I pulled out of her, hearing a thankful gasp of relief as she felt me leaving her.

"Go," I said, and she didn't need to be told twice.

She climbed out of the sunken tub, not even bothering with the steps. She half crawled across the floor, only getting to her feet at the edge of the raised dais that held the toilet. She looked at me with wide eyes, as if in horror.

"You're going to watch?"

"Now," I told her sternly. "Don't make me tell you again."

I saw the flush of humiliation in her face, the glow of arousal that accompanied it. She let herself go with a long, low moan, and her great gasping breaths teetered right on the edge of sobs.

She panted heavily as she sat on the toilet, embarrassed and aroused.

I watched her wipe herself, looking shyly and sheepishly over at me. My urge to look away was conquered only with great effort. She had one thing right: this was utter debauchery. We had just crossed the final taboo, the squick to end all squicks. The humiliation in Jolie's face was evident—but when she returned to me and I slid my fingers between her legs, she was wetter than ever, and not from the water.

"Now the fun starts," I said with a wink.

Jolie was positioned in a receptive position on the bed. Pillows were tucked under her belly, her ass thrust high in the air. She had spread her legs very wide, something at which she excelled.

I had taken a moment to wash up, soaping and rinsing my cock—you never know where you're going to want to put such a thing. She had looked back at me as I returned to the bedroom, begging me with those green eyes, one finger in her mouth being bitten coquettishly.

Now I took off my swimsuit, knelt behind her on the bed, and put on my gloves. The two snapping sounds they made sent a shiver through my naked supplicant.

My hands sheathed in rubber, I started by fingering her pussy.

It was still wet, wetter than ever, but the glove required lube. I slid two, then three fingers in deeply, feeling the swell of her G-spot against the pads of my fingers. I let my thumb rest against her clit, working it as I fucked her with my left hand.

She would have climaxed the first time before I even entered her ass, if I hadn't heard the timbre of her moans and backed off. I wanted her right on the edge when I took her, when I felt my hand sliding all the way into her ass.

I withdrew my hand from inside her and squeezed out a healthy dollop of lube onto the fingers of my right hand—the enema, of course, had washed away every bit of lube.

Her asshole was tight at first, her ordeal with the water having pulled her muscles into a knot. One finger was the most it felt like I could ever get into her—and I began to wish I'd fucked her first, sliding my cock in to sample that exquisitely snug entrance.

But she opened up quickly, one finger easily becoming two, then with more lube, three. Again I had to back off to keep her from coming. She bit her lip to try to hide her moans. I knew she wanted me to let her come. But I could read her, and I let her cool down before adding more lube.

"Ask for it," I told her.

She had to fumble for the words, her voice hoarse with arousal.

"Please put your hand in my ass," she said softly. "Sir."

"Do you still want it?"

She tucked her head girlishly to one side and looked back at me. I met her eyes and saw the sensuality in her red-smeared lips as she formed the words.

"More than anything."

So I gave her four fingers, twisting my hand in a well-lubricated corkscrew, and she cried out and cursed, whimpering and moaning. There were three in her pussy, then two, then three, a thumb on her clit and her orgasm coming closer. She pushed herself back against me. She knew the feel of it from being fisted before. Only this time, it wasn't her pussy that I was taking with my hand.

"How—how many is—is—" she stammered, turning her head to look at me, her eyes rolling crazily.

"Four," I told her. "You want it?"

"Please," she said. "Please fist my ass, Sir. Fuck, you have big fuckin' hands."

I raised my eyebrows, and she added urgently: "Sir."

I went back to three fingers and two, working her rhythmically open as her arousal mounted. She could come any time now. I *wanted* her to come. But I wanted her surrender more than I wanted her orgasm. I added more lube and returned my fourth finger to her ass.

The time to finger her pussy was finished. I needed both my hands, now. As I had when I'd fisted her cunt, I slid one finger of my left hand in alongside the four of my right. She had to struggle to take it, but she pushed herself onto me. An hour had passed now, with her on the edge and her ass slowly opening up to accommodate me. I had toyed with the idea of fisting her pussy before her ass. But I knew that even for a slut like Jolie, it might be more than she could take.

"How—how many is that?" she gasped.

"Five," I said. "But not the whole fist."

"Fuck. Fuck, fuck, Sir, I think your hands are too big."

"All right," I said, and slid the extra finger out, then slowly began to withdraw, corkscrew-fashion.

"No," she said. "I—I think I can take it."

"You *think* you can take it," I growled.

That was all it required. The sound of my low, domineering growl, the hint of displeasure mingling with the sense of total ownership, told her everything she needed to know. If I hadn't heard it in her next words, I would have seen it in her eyes—she wanted me to push her.

"I can take it," she said. "Please. Put it in."

"You'll take it," I growled, and the soft moan she gave as I returned my four fingers to her ass was music—music, I tell you—to my ears.

"Thank you, Sir," she mewled. "Thank you for making me take your fist in my ass." Her voice got softer as she lost herself in the sensations, as I added more lube and gently fucked four fingers into her. "Please, Sir," she whispered. "Please, Sir, fist my ass. Please, Sir, fucking fist my ass with your big fucking hands—oh!"

The thumb had joined the four fingers, conjuring a yelp from Jolie. Not the fist, yet—just the tip of the thumb, my hand in classic duck-bill shape as I pushed up to my knuckles and felt the cinch of her asshole around my hand.

"Please, Sir," she begged. "Please put your fist in my ass."

More lube—I was on the third tube. I twisted my fingers in a slow half-circle, forward, back, forward, back, feeling her asshole relax as I told her "rub your clit."

She obediently reached down, began to stroke herself, letting out a cry of pleasure as her hand worked her own clit.

"Push yourself onto me."

As she worked her hips, pushing herself back against my hand, her asshole relaxed further, and I twisted, slowly, adding more lube, opening her up with a series of gentle thrusts.

Then, like a mouth opening to say the words *fuck me,* her asshole just *gave,* accepting my hand past the knuckles, in a sudden tight grasp that drew me in, up to the wrist, bringing a wail of invective from Jolie.

"Fuck! Fuck! Fuck! Fuck!"

I asked her if she was all right. She said she didn't know.

Then, not an instant later, she pushed back onto me, hard, letting out a moan that was so close to a scream that the distinction didn't matter—to anyone except, maybe, our neighbors.

"Fuck, fuck, fuck, fuck, fuck," she moaned. "Fuck that feels good—I'm going to…"

Her words trailed off; her experience was so far beyond language that nothing could have said it. Her asshole seemed to relax another notch, and she pushed herself hard onto my hand, burying me just beyond the wrist in her asshole. Even Jolie must have known that it wasn't going in any deeper—the tightness was clear. But still she fucked herself fervently, almost violently, onto my fist.

Her hand had left her clit. She gripped the edge of the bed, pushing herself against me, *fucking* herself against my hand, and with a scream that didn't even begin to sound like a moan, she came. Her asshole clenched in rhythmic spasms, my hand and hers far away from her clit, from her pussy. She came from being fisted alone, and if volume was any indication, this was not your garden-variety orgasm. By the time she'd finished thrashing and clawing, impaled on my fist, the already damp and dirty sheets were ruined, not just tangled but torn, and she'd ripped a hole in the pillowcase with her teeth.

I'd been so bewitched by her motions and her screams that I hadn't even noticed the wet spurts that now darkened the bed. Jolie lay bent over, her fisted ass high in the air, her legs splayed at an improbable angle, her mouth uttering incoherent moans.

"I'm going to take it out, now," I said. "Push out, very gently."

Removing my fist from Jolie's ass was a tall order, though. Her orgasm had tightened her muscles around my wrist, and my hand was already asleep. By the time I'd exerted even the gentlest of pressures, she was begging for more. She didn't *want* it out. She wanted me to fist her deeper.

She didn't say the words, but I did, "I think it's time for *both* hands," and that's when she came the second time, gently rocking my fist back and forth in her asshole, her muscles going crazy as they assaulted my wrist. By the time she was finished, then, I was able to gently twist my hand, add more lube, ease back a little, very gently; very, very gently; every motion bringing a twitch from Jolie's naked body, her limbs shaking. Still she begged for more.

When my fist finally popped out of her ass, I heard Jolie sobbing—and while I knew that it was just the emotional catharsis that so often accompanies being fisted, I'll admit I was more than a little flattered. I slipped off the glove, inverted it, and tossed it on the floor. I crawled up alongside Jolie and held her while she sobbed.

The room had gone dark, our two—or was it three?—hour session of anal fisting having taken us well into the early evening. It was time for dinner, and I could feel my stomach grumbling. But Jolie was still crying, and I suspected that even Panamanian pastries wouldn't stop her.

"Is it a bad cry or a good cry?" I asked her, feeling oddly embarrassed to be asking such a wussy question at the close of such a session. I knew, usually, what the crying was about— fisting is one of those things, sometimes, that makes a girl cry, for no reason other than that she has just been fisted.

But I'd been misled, you might say, by the fact that when I fisted her pussy, all Jolie had done was moan and come and squirt—and beg for more.

She was too far gone to answer me, anyway. She just cried and cuddled close to me. But any fear I might have had that I'd gone too far was salved when, still crying, she kissed her way down my body and took my cock in her mouth, sucking me with little whimpers and moans and sobs, her flowing tears warm on my flesh. It might have embarrassed me that, all while she was crying, my cock had never lost its hardness. It might have embarrassed me—if my cock had been in anyone's mouth other than Jolie's.

Her lips clamped halfway down my shaft, she drank me, swallowing my come as her well-ravaged ass wriggled fetchingly back and forth. When she squirmed back up alongside me, wrapping herself around my naked body, she wasn't crying anymore.

She was calling me Sir, thanking me, and begging again. This time, for room service.

WORTH IT

Alison Tyler

As the ring slid onto my finger, I knew it was all over. The sparkle of diamonds glinting in the dim candlelight. The pink tourmaline shining like a flame. Those jewels foretold our demise as clearly as any fortune-teller could have. I knew the end was inevitable, even if I didn't know why. Well, that's not altogether true. I knew, sort of. I knew in a half-assed, bitchy kind of way.

A week before, Byron had taken me on a dream shopping spree to Tiffany & Co., had told me to choose the ring I desired the most. "Go for it, Gina. Pick out the one you love." What girl wouldn't melt at an opportunity like that?

Flustered, flattered, I'd landed on this one after nearly an hour of breathless searching. Or, at least, one damn near like it. Dramatically dark pink stone in the center, two perfect diamonds on either side, a classic platinum band. Admittedly, the price was astronomical, but Byron had the money for the ring. And I was worth it, right?

Apparently not.

This ring did not come in the pretty pale blue box that makes all women's hearts skip a beat, but in a knockoff lavender velvet container, from a knockoff jewelry store in West L.A. *This* ring cost five hundred dollars instead of twelve thousand dollars. And I should have been happy with whatever Byron gave me. I know that. But like a bossy five year old who throws a tantrum at her own birthday party, I was not happy at all. Because it was clear to me from the look in his watery green eyes as they carefully appraised my reaction that I wasn't worth it.

Like I wasn't worth a lot of things.

I wasn't worth kissing in public. ("PDAs are *so* revolting.") I wasn't worth risking potential shame or embarrassment in the back row of a movie theater. ("*Stop that*, Gina. People might see.") I wasn't worth trying something new in bed, even though Byron had dabbled in adventurous sex with girls before me. But no matter how I cajoled, he wouldn't travel uncharted territory on our California King.

Velvety handcuffs? No.

A leopard-print blindfold? No f-ing way.

He'd had *anal* sex before me, twice, with a girl he met in New York City. I knew this because early in our relationship, when we'd been in that cozy sharing place that happens prior to going long-term, he'd confessed. I'd told him that I'd lost my virginity to a frat boy whom I chose to do the honors because he put his arms around me on a balcony during a party to keep me warm. Chivalry had gotten him where no man had before. We retreated to my dorm room twin bed and he'd made me come twice while sixty-nining.

Byron had countered with his tale of debauchery in New York City. He'd bragged about the act, as if it were something he did every day. But as the story continued, I deduced that playing this way had been entirely the girl's idea. He'd simply gone along with the concept, taking down her jeans, bending her over the hotel bed, fucking her *there*. I don't actually think he enjoyed the act—too dirty for Byron, who liked things antiseptically clean, from missionary-style sex in our king-sized bed to the grout between the white tiles in the bathroom. Still, he held the experience close to his heart, like a badge of courage. It was a medal of sexual adventurousness for a Boy Scout like him.

Whenever we made love after that, I thought of the girl. She had blonde hair, cut short and spiky. She wore sunglasses even inside, and she liked to chew Double-Bubble gum. There were pictures of her in his scrapbook, black-and-white photos of her blowing bubbles, of her winking at him, of her with her hand in the belt loop of her jeans, looking oh so cocky.

What did she have to look cocky about?

Simply this: she'd had Byron in a way I couldn't.

In truth, I hadn't had sex like that with anyone. I was only nineteen. My experiences were limited. Even frat boys who are willing to sixty-nine for hours don't always broach the taboo topic of anal sex. I wished I'd done it, though. Knowing that Byron had ass-fucked someone else made me feel uneven with him, as if he were winning. As if he'd *always* be winning.

So I asked him to do it to me. To take down *my* jeans. To bend *me* over.

"Uh-uh," he said, shaking his head. "You won't like it."

Why? Why wouldn't I like it?

"It'll hurt."

"We can use K-Y."

"It's—it's dirty, Gina."

He said the word in a way that made me know he thought *dirty* was bad. But to me, the thought of getting Byron to do something dirty couldn't have been sexier. Mess him up. That's what I wanted to do. Rumple him around the edges. Untuck the hospital corners on his highly starched personality.

"Come on," I urged him. "You've done it before. You know how."

"Kiddo," he said in his most condescending voice. "Trust me. It's not for you."

Byron was nearly thirty. You'd have thought he would enjoy introducing me to new things, but aside from training me in which brands he preferred for toothpaste (Crest), mouthwash (Scope), and soap (Dial)—the types his mommy always bought— he claimed that he wasn't much of a teacher.

Yet I desired knowledge. I craved experience. Now that Byron wouldn't even consider having anal sex with me, it was all that I wanted. I started to think about my ass in a way that I never had before. To consider my behind as a sexual object in its own right.

Although I'd always been in favor of hipster panties, or (at the skimpiest) bikinis, I now bought myself a rainbow of thongs, and I twitched my ass in them when I walked, feeling that ribbon of floss tickling me with every step. Opening me up.

When I took a shower, I took great pleasure in using the pulsating massager between my rear cheeks rather than over my clit. The rush of water there had me breathless and shaking as I'd never been before. And when I touched myself solo, I'd finger my ass simultaneously, and my orgasms intensified in ways I'd never imagined. Nobody had told me. Nobody had explained.

Maybe, I thought, Byron needed to see what it would feel like. Maybe nobody had told *him*, either. The next time we made love, I tried to touch him back there, but he swatted my hand away, and the lovemaking stopped abruptly. How could I consider that? How could I dream he'd be into *that*? When I went down on him soon after, something he *did* like, I tried accidentally-on-purpose to kiss him back there, slipping lower between his legs than normal, but he pulled me back up to his cock, horrified that I would even consider rimming him.

The more he denied me, the more I craved what I couldn't have.

How strange that something I'd never known I wanted now consumed me. I dreamed about him taking my ass. I wanted him to pound into me. I felt as if I were on fire all the time, felt as if the curves of my ass were a beacon, a neon sign, pulsing. Throbbing. And was I just imagining things, or were other people suddenly realizing how cool my ass was? I wore tighter jeans. I wore shorter, flirtier skirts. Byron's best friend, Joshua, seemed to notice. On a day when I wore Daisy Duke cutoffs, he couldn't keep his eyes off me. But Byron was oblivious.

I was determined to wake him up.

Whenever I felt the mood was right, I'd try to perk Byron up to the concept. I'd ask him to play with me the way he'd played with Vacation Girl, the trippy little blonde-haired minx in the Vuarnet shades who'd let him take her from behind. But what did I know? Maybe she'd taken *him*. Maybe she'd fucked him from below.

"Come on," I begged yet again one evening after a party. We were both tipsy, but I acted a little more drunk than I really felt. "Come on, Byron, let's try it."

By then he knew exactly what I meant. We'd had this conversation often enough for him to know what "it" was. His face squinched up. He shook his head. He looked as if he'd just taken a bite of something rotten.

"I want to," I told him, giving him my most desirous look. Lashes fluttering. Bottom lip in a bitable pout.

"No," he said, in a tone that let me know he was gearing up for a fight. "No way."

Although I hadn't given the concept of anal sex much thought before Byron and I got together, now I had discovered that I really *did* want to. Men had been complimenting my ass for years. Since high school, even. Boys who suddenly realized that they weren't breast men, but ass men, took an extra look at my derriere when I walked by. Did anything come between me and *my* Calvins? That's what the boys wanted to know. Byron had that ass in his very own bed, and he wouldn't glance at it twice.

How crazy it is that I begged. How pathetic that I had to go that low.

He'd fucked *her* that way. It was all I could think about. *She* got him to do it. She wouldn't take no for an answer.

I got drunk again. Drunker this time. But I was prepared. I'd purchased a bottle of glistening lube. I unfurled a fresh towel and spread the blue terry cloth out on the bed while Byron was in the adjoining bathroom, brushing his teeth. My body, ass included, was squeaky clean from a shower. I was Crested, Scoped, and Dialed, as tempting as I could possibly manage. Somewhere in the back of my head, I knew that most men would have dived at the opportunity of doing me the way I craved. Young chicklet on the bed, ass up, ready for sex.

Byron said no.

He didn't want to do the act with the girl he would marry. That's what it all came down to. He tried to make it seem as if he were sparing *me* an indignity. Really, I could tell the truth was a different story entirely. I wasn't worth it. The fight that followed was groundbreaking. Byron didn't like me arguing with him about anything, and he punished me by leaving the apartment, storming out to have a cool-down walk in the night air.

All by myself, and drunker still, I looked at the photos from his vacation in New York, the one he'd gone on with Joshua

after finishing graduate school. The one where he'd met the girl.
I saw her gazing from under her shades, saw her daring me.

I took that dare.

What I did was indefensible. What I did was wrong, wrong,
wrong. What I did wasn't actually a *what* but a *who*—Joshua
Sparks, Byron's best friend.

I didn't start up with the "fuck my ass" request immediately.
I simply began responding to the flirtatiousness in Josh's dark
brown eyes whenever we were together. I held his interested
stare a beat too long. Whenever we talked, I put my hand on his
shoulder, or thigh, or the inside of his wrist. At parties, I stood
too close. At dinners, I always sat across from him, and my
stockinged toes did naughty things between his legs from under
the table.

Josh started calling when he knew Byron wasn't going to be
around. "Hey, Gina, is Byron there?"

"No, Josh."

"Good—"

He wanted me to talk dirty to him when he was at work.
"Tell me what you want," he'd demand. "Tell me everything."

"You first," I'd counter.

He wanted me to watch him jerk off.

I could do that.

He wanted me to give him a blow job in his car, during rush
hour.

I could do that, too.

He wanted me every which way he could get me. At least,
that's what he promised. "Every which way—and then all those
ways again."

But would he fulfill my one true desire? That was the question. Or would he make me beg the way I had begged Byron,

my fingers on the split of my ass, ready to open myself up to him? Would he make me beg, and then reject me? I didn't think I could handle that.

When Josh and I finally got together after all those months of dancing around the issue, I didn't know how to ask. I simply rolled over in bed and bumped him from behind.

"Byron won't," I told him. "I've asked, and he won't."

"Why not?" His strong fingertips lingered between my ass-cheeks. He touched me more firmly and I shuddered all over. "Why, Gina?" I looked at my ring, glinting at me accusingly from the bedside table. I looked over my shoulder at Josh. "Why do you want to so bad?" he asked, amending his original question.

"Because he won't." I'd built the act into something else in my mind. A super hurdle. Something to overcome.

Josh didn't want me to see it like that. He wanted me not to get over it, but to revel in every single second. He didn't want me to beg him to fuck my ass, he wanted me to beg him not to stop. He explained this to me as he touched my naked skin, humbling me with the sensation of his fingers spreading me apart. Making my heart race faster as he inspected me. And suddenly I didn't want him to fuck me there just because Byron wouldn't. I wanted him to fuck my ass because I needed him to. I wanted him to drive inside of me, to make me scream, to make me feel as if he were fucking me all the way through my body.

Josh knew what he was doing. There was plenty of lube and there was lots of stroking. He slid in one finger. Then two.

"Oh, yes," I sighed. "Oh, Josh."

He finger-fucked my ass as he rubbed my clit with his free hand. My body responded instantly. I felt the wetness spreading down my legs as my pussy grew steadily more aroused. He dribbled the shivery cold lube down the split between my cheeks until it rained onto the crisp sheets. He made me come before he even brought his cock to my hole. He made me come again with only the very head of it inside of me.

"Oh, god," I murmured, undone by the feeling. "Oh, fucking god—"

He kissed the back of my neck as he worked me, and when he slid in all the way, I bit into the pillow and cried.

Byron was wrong. Yeah, it hurt, but it hurt in the best way possible. It hurt like nothing else ever had, and the pleasure of being filled was like no other experience. I didn't want it to stop. I didn't want it to end.

I thought about Byron denying me this. I thought about the spiky-haired blonde and her "I dare you" stare. And then I came again, as the diamonds made dizzy, drunken rainbows from my knockoff ring on the bedside table.

I tried to make myself feel bad for leaving Byron. I told myself I ought to have at least a twinge of guilty conscience over it. But the truth is this: he simply wasn't worth it.

ANAL SEX IN MONTMARTRE

Lavie Tidhar

The Seine rushes through your orifices
In a quiet, rhythmic motion

Like the breaking of waves against your skin
Against your dam, the color of night over Place Pigalle

Like a Renaissance drawing, anatomic and precise
Of a conjoined machine made flesh.

The ghosts of courtesans and faded gentlemen
Whisper around us as the dirty moon reflects in the Seine:

There is something decidedly romantic
Decidedly *parisienne* about our movements.

It is that feeling
How you say in French.

ABOUT THE AUTHORS

XAVIER ACTON's work has appeared at Gothic.net and in *Good Vibrations* magazine and many anthologies, including *MASTER*, Violet Blue's *Sweet Life* series and *Taboo*, and the *Naughty Stories from A to Z* series. Acton lives in California, where he is at work on an erotic horror novel.

After discovering the intriguing possibilities of a bare water bed, three gallons of baby oil, and a good running start, **CHRIS BRIDGES** has devoted his life to silly sex in all its forms. Collections of his findings may be seen at HootIsland.com—the only island with an anti-dress code—or in his collection *Giggling Into the Pillow*, available at fine online bookstores everywhere.

FELIX D'ANGELO writes erotica to share with his lovers and occasionally for publication. His work has appeared in Violet Blue's *Sweet Life* series and several other anthologies.

DANTE DAVIDSON is a tenured professor in Santa Barbara, California. His short stories have appeared in *Bondage, Naughty Stories from A to Z, Best Bondage Erotica, The Merry XXXmas Book of Erotica,* and *Sweet Life.* With Alison Tyler, he is the coauthor of the best-selling collection of short fiction *Bondage on a Budget* and *Secrets for Great Sex After Fifty* (which he wrote at age twenty-eight).

KATE DOMINIC (www.katedominic.com) is the author of *Any 2 People, Kissing,* which was a finalist for the 2004 Foreword Magazine Book of the Year Award in the short story category. Kate has published over three hundred erotic short stories, writing under a variety of pen names in both female and male voices. Her most recent work is available in *Best of Best Women's Erotica, Glamour Girls, Naughty Spanking Stories from A-Z, The Many Joys of Sex Toys, Dyke the Halls,* and *Ultimate Lesbian Erotica 2004.* Kate's column "The Business End" appears monthly at the Erotica Readers & Writers Association (www.erotica-readers.com). She is a featured monthly writer at Lady Susan's "A Private Affair" (www.spanking-lifestyle.com).

ERICA DUMAS's short erotica has appeared in the *Sweet Life* series, the *Naughty Stories from A to Z* series, and numerous other anthologies. She lives with her lover in Southern California, where she is currently at work on a short-story collection and an erotic novel. She can be contacted at ericamdumas@yahoo.com.

SHANNA GERMAIN makes her living by writing about many topics, but desire is definitely her favorite. If you desire to read more of her work, you can find it in books like *Cheeky, The Good Parts, Heat Wave, Dykes on Bikes,* and *Rode Hard, Put Away Wet,* and on her website, www.shannagermain.com.

BRYN HANIVER loves the ocean and writes from islands and peninsulas on both sides of North America—with occasional stints in the Caribbean. Previous anthology credits include *Delicate Friction* and *A Taste of Midnight*.

MICHAEL HEMMINGSON lives in San Diego, shuttling from Encinitas, Borrego Springs, and Ocean Beach. His most recent books are *Expelled from Eden: A William T. Vollmann Reader*; *In the Background Is a Walled City*; *The Las Vegas Quartet*; and *The Yacht People*.

CARL KENNEDY is the pseudonym of a well-known writer who occasionally dabbles in erotica to record his most exorbitant sexual adventures.

MARILYN JAYE LEWIS's erotic short stories and novellas have been widely anthologized in the United States and Europe. Her erotic romance novels include *When Hearts Collide, In the Secret Hours,* and *When the Night Stood Still.* She is the editor of a number of erotic short-story anthologies, including *Stirring Up a Storm.* Upcoming novels include *Twilight of the Immortal, Killing on Mercy Road,* and *Freak Parade.*

N. T. MORLEY is the author of more than a dozen published novels of dominance and submission, including *The Parlor, The Limousine, The Circle, The Nightclub, The Appointment,* and the trilogies *The Library, The Castle,* and *The Office.* Morley has also edited two anthologies, *MASTER* and *slave.*

JOLIE DU PRÉ's erotica appears on the Internet, in e-book format, and in print in *Hot & Bothered 4, Down and Dirty* Volume 2, and *Best Bondage Erotica 2.*

AYRE RILEY has written for *Down & Dirty*, *Naughty Stories from A to Z* Volume 3, *Taboo*, and *Slave*.

JEAN ROBERTA teaches English in a Canadian prairie university and writes erotica, reviews, articles, and rants. Her stories have appeared in over twenty anthologies, including *Best Lesbian Erotica* (2000, 2001, 2004, and 2005) and *Best Women's Erotica* (2000, 2003, 2005, and 2006). Her lesbian e-novel, *Prairie Gothic*, is available from Amatory Ink (www.amatory-ink.co.uk). Check out her column, "In My Jeans," on www.bluefood.com.

THOMAS S. ROCHE's more than three hundred published short stories and three hundred published articles have appeared in a wide variety of magazines, anthologies, and websites. In addition, his ten published books include *His* and *Hers*, two books of erotica coauthored with Alison Tyler, as well as three volumes of the *Noirotica* series. He has recently taken up erotic photography, which he showcases at his website, www.skidroche.com.

JOY ST. JAMES is an East Coast writer and editor. Her erotica, under her former byline Joy James, has appeared in numerous print anthologies and websites. Despite her recent name change, she doesn't pretend to be a saint, but remains, happily as always, a slut, literary and otherwise. Joy can be reached at joyce.james@att.net.

DOMINIC SANTI is a former technical editor turned rogue whose erotic stories have appeared in dozens of anthologies and magazines, including *Best American Erotica 2004*; *Best Gay Erotica 2000* and *2004*; *Best of Best Gay Erotica 2*; *Freshmen: The Best*; *His Underwear*; and many volumes of *Friction*. Santi's latest book is the German collection *Kerle im Lustrausch (Horny Guys)*. www.nicksantistories.com

TRISTAN TAORMINO (www.puckerup.com) is too busy for her own good. She is the author of three books: *True Lust: Adventures in Sex, Porn and Perversion*; *Down and Dirty Sex Secrets*; and *The Ultimate Guide to Anal Sex for Women*, a new, revised edition of which was published in January 2006. She is series editor of *Best Lesbian Erotica*, which has won two Lambda Literary Awards. She is director, producer and star of the award-winning videos *Tristan Taormino's Ultimate Guide to Anal Sex for Women 1 and 2*, distributed by Evil Angel Video, and she recently completed a new video, *Tristan Taormino's House of Ass*, which was released in January 2006 by Adam & Eve Pictures. She is the sex columnist for the *Village Voice*, a columnist for *Taboo* and *Velvetpark*, and the former editor of *On Our Backs*. She lives with her partner and their three dogs in New York City.

LAVIE TIDHAR's erotic poetry has appeared in *Moist* magazine, *The International Journal of Erotica*, and the anthology *Velvet Heat*; other poems have appeared in UK magazines such as *Cadenza, Dream Catcher*, and *Brittle Star*. An early collection of his Hebrew poetry, *Remnants of God,* was published in 1998, and he was the winner of the undergraduate James Ragan poetry prize in 2002.

SAGE VIVANT operates Custom Erotica Source, where she and her staff of writers craft tailor-made erotic fiction for individual clients. She is the editor of *Swing!* and coeditor with M. Christian of *Confessions: Admissions of Sexual Guilt*; *The Best of Both Worlds: Bisexual Erotica*; *Leather, Lace, and Lust*; and *Amazons: Sexy Tales of Strong Women*. Her work has appeared in dozens of anthologies and she is the author of *29 Ways to Write Great Erotica*, available at www.customeroticasource.com.

SASKIA WALKER (www.saskiawalker.co.uk) is a British author who has had short erotic fiction published on both sides of the pond. You can find her work in *Seductions: Tales of Erotic Persuasion*; *Sugar and Spice*; *More Wicked Words*; *Wicked Words 5* and *8*; *Naughty Stories from A to Z* volumes 3 and 4; *Naked Erotica*; *Taboo: Forbidden Fantasies For Couples*; *Three-Way*; *Best Bondage Erotica 2*; *The Merry XXXmas Book of Erotica*; *Sextopia*; *Stolen Moments: Erotic Interludes*; *Best Women's Erotica 2006*; and *Stirring Up a Storm*. She also writes erotic romance and in 2005 published her first novel, *Along for the Ride,* and a novella entitled *Summer Lightning*.

GREG WHARTON is the author of *Johnny Was & Other Tall Tales*. He is also the editor of numerous anthologies, including the Lambda Literary Award–winning *I Do/I Don't: Queers on Marriage* (coedited with Ian Philips). He lives in San Francisco with his brilliant and sexy husband Ian, a cat named Chloe, and a lot of books.

ERIC WILLIAMS is a Los Angeles–based writer. His short stories have appeared in several *Penthouse* publications.

ABOUT THE EDITOR

Called "a trollop with a laptop" by *East Bay Express*, **ALISON TYLER** is naughty and she knows it. Over the past decade, Ms. Tyler has written more than fifteen explicit novels, including *Learning to Love It*, *Strictly Confidential*, *Sweet Thing*, *Sticky Fingers*, and *Something About Workmen* (all published by Black Lace), as well as *Rumours* and the forthcoming *Tiffany Twisted* (Cheek). Her novels have been translated into Japanese, Dutch, German, Norwegian, and Spanish. Her stories have appeared in anthologies, including *Sweet Life* and *Sweet Life 2*, *Taboo*, *Best Women's Erotica* (2002, 2003, 2005, and 2006), *Best of Best Women's Erotica*, *Best Fetish Erotica*, and *Best Lesbian Erotica 1996* (all published by Cleis), and in *Wicked Words* (4, 5, 6, 8, and 10), *Sex on Holiday*, *Sex at the Office*, and *Sex in Uniform* (Black Lace), as well as in *Playgirl* magazine.

She is the editor of *Batteries Not Included* (Diva); *Heat Wave*, *Best Bondage Erotica* volumes 1 and 2, *Three-Way*, and *The Merry XXXmas Book of Erotica* (all from Cleis Press); and the *Naughty Stories from A to Z* series, the *Down & Dirty* series, *Naked Erotica,* and *Juicy Erotica* (all from Pretty Things Press). Please visit www.prettythingspress.com.

The only unnatural sexual act is that which you cannot perform.
                              —ALFRED KINSEY (1894–1956)

More Bestselling Erotica from Alison Tyler

Buy 4 books,
Get 1 FREE*

Ordering is easy!

Call us toll free to place your MC/VISA order or mail the order form below with payment to: Cleis Press, PO Box 14697, San Francisco, CA 94114.

ORDER FORM

QTY	TITLE	PRICE

SUBTOTAL _____

SHIPPING _____

SALES TAX _____

TOTAL _____

Add $3.95 postage/handling for the first book ordered and $1.00 for each additional book. Outside North America, please contact us for shipping rates. California residents add 8.5% sales tax. Payment in U.S. dollars only.

* Free book of equal or lesser value. Shipping and applicable sales tax extra.
Cleis Press • (800) 780-2279 • orders@cleispress.com
www.cleispress.com